PUFFIN BOOKS

HEART OF ICE

Louise Cooper was born in Hertfordshire in 1952. She hated school so much – spending most lessons clandestinely writing stories – that she persuaded her parents to let her abandon her education at the age of fifteen and has never regretted it. Her first novel was published when she was twenty. She moved to London in 1975 and worked in publishing before becoming a full-time writer in 1977. Since then she has published more than twenty fantasy novels, for both adults and children, and has ideas for many more to come. She also writes occasional short stories, and poetry for her own pleasure.

Louise Cooper lives in an area sandwiched between the Cotswolds and the Malverns and gains a great deal of inspiration from the scenery. She is also potty about cats and steam trains!

Heart of Ice was previously published as *The Hounds of Winter* in the Dark Enchantment series.

Some other books by Louise Cooper

HEART OF DUST
HEART OF FIRE
HEART OF GLASS

Heart of Ice

Louise Cooper

PUFFIN BOOKS

PUFFIN BOOKS

Published by the Penguin Group
Penguin Books Ltd, 27 Wrights Lane, London W8 5TZ, England
Penguin Putnam Inc., 375 Hudson Street, New York, New York 10014, USA
Penguin Books Australia Ltd, Ringwood, Victoria, Australia
Penguin Books Canada Ltd, 10 Alcorn Avenue, Toronto, Ontario, Canada M4V 3B2
Penguin Books (NZ) Ltd, 182–190 Wairau Road, Auckland 10, New Zealand

Penguin Books Ltd, Registered Offices: Harmondsworth, Middlesex, England

First published in Puffin Books 1996
Reissued in this edition 1998
1 3 5 7 9 10 8 6 4 2

Typeset in 12/15 Plantin

Made and printed in England by Clays Ltd, St Ives plc

British Library Cataloguing in Publication Data
A CIP catalogue record for this book is available from the British Library

ISBN 0–140–38770–6

Chapter One

A T THE MOMENT when Silvan put the ring on Tavia's finger, Jansie simply couldn't bear to watch but turned her head away, furiously biting back the tears. *Silvan doesn't love me*, she told herself. *He loves my sister, and today is their wedding day, and I must forget my dreams!*

The priest spoke the final words, and a little sigh went through the gathering of family and friends. Husband and wife. Silvan and Tavia. And as she looked at the tall, dark, gauntly handsome figure of her new brother-in-law, Jansie felt as if a knife had stabbed into her heart.

With the ceremony over, the celebration began. The house had been decorated with ribbons, garlands and good-luck symbols; a hundred candles burned in the great hall, and everywhere was brightness and laughter. All Jansie's relations had come, uncles and aunts and cousins, and many friends besides; enough people to make up for the fact that Silvan had no family of his own. Later there was music and dancing, and soon after the dancing began, Jansie's cousin Issa found Jansie sitting alone on the landing that overlooked the great staircase.

'Oh, Jansie!' Issa crouched down, her face sympathetic and concerned. 'Please don't cry.'

'I'm not crying,' Jansie said fiercely. But it wasn't true; tears were glittering on her eyelashes.

'It's Silvan, isn't it?' Issa sighed. 'The

trouble is, I think every girl who ever sets eyes on him must fall in love with him.'

'Don't tell Tavia, Issa, please don't!' Jansie pleaded. 'I don't want to spoil her day.'

'Of course I won't tell her,' Issa said. She knew how fond Jansie and Tavia had always been of each other.

'And I am being foolish, I know,' Jansie went on mournfully. 'Tavia's three years older than me, and Silvan's older still. I'm too young for him – Mother says I shouldn't even be thinking about marriage until I'm at least seventeen, and that's two years away. But oh, Issa, it doesn't stop me *wishing*.'

'I know.' Issa sighed again. Then, trying to buoy Jansie with a wry joke, she added, 'Perhaps Silvan has a younger brother? Or two would be better – then we could have one each!'

Jansie almost managed to laugh, then shook her head. 'Silvan hasn't got any family at all.' And she thought silently,

Except for Tavia. She's his family now. And tonight she'll go away with him, away to his house, where they'll both be so far from me . . .

'Come on,' Issa said, seeing that Jansie was about to cry again. 'You mustn't go back with red eyes and blotchy cheeks, or Tavia will know that you're upset. Let me dab your face – there, that's better – and we'll go downstairs together.'

She pulled her cousin to her feet and linked arms firmly with her. 'You'll get over him, Jansie. You will.'

The carriage that was to take Silvan and Tavia away to their new life was at the door shortly after sunset. All the guests gathered on the steps to wish them Godspeed on their four-day journey, and Tavia, radiant and laughing, swept Jansie into her arms.

'Oh, Jansie, this has been such a wonderful day!' Tavia hugged her sister tightly. 'Now, you'll come and see us soon, won't you? Promise?'

4

'I promise. As soon as you want me to come, just write to me.' And Jansie meant it. For until she was invited, until that letter came, there would be no chance to see Silvan again.

Then Silvan stepped forward. He took Jansie's hands in his and she felt a thrill rush through her fingers, through her arms, into her heart. She looked up at his face, at the fine bones, the frame of black hair with the strange but distinguishing white streak at the temples. Into his vivid green eyes . . .

Silvan smiled at her, a smile that devastated her soul. 'Goodbye, dear sister Jansie,' he said. And Jansie's dreams collapsed and blew away on the late summer breeze. *Sister*. That was all she was to him, all she would ever be. He loved Tavia. And that hurt so much.

She heard the carriage door close, heard the coachman call to the horses – 'Come *hup*!' – and the crack of the whip. Hoofs clattered, the carriage wheels rumbled, and Silvan and Tavia were

5

carried away into the gathering night.

Jansie went up to her bedroom. The festivities were still in full swing and would go on until past midnight, but she couldn't bear to join in any more. She closed her door and sat down in front of her looking-glass, gazing at her own face. Her hair wasn't golden like Tavia's, but only brown. And her eyes were not blue, only hazel. *Tavia is beautiful*, Jansie thought, *and I'm not*. Little wonder that Silvan had fallen in love with her sister. Little wonder that he would never dream of looking twice at Jansie.

Suddenly Jansie couldn't face the glass any more. She ran to her bed, threw herself down on the familiar, friendly counterpane, and sobbed herself to sleep.

Tavia wrote once to say that she and Silvan had arrived safely, and then there was no further letter for months. Summer gave way to autumn and autumn to winter, and still no word came. Jansie fretted more and more each week, until her father despaired of her and even her mother declared that she was becoming 'quite impossible!'

Then, a few days after the Midwinter Solstice, a letter came. It wasn't brought by the usual post-runner but by a fair-haired boy some two or three years older than Jansie, who rode up to the door on a stout pony one brisk, chilly morning. The boy's name was Gilmer, he said; he was in service at Silvan's house and his master had asked him to carry this message. Jansie barely gave the young messenger a second glance; she was too excited and eager to know what Tavia had to say.

But the letter wasn't from Tavia. It was from Silvan himself. He had to go away on business, he said, and would be absent from home until spring. He was worried that Tavia would be lonely, and so he wondered if Jansie might wish to stay at his house during his absence, to keep her sister company.

Jansie was thrilled by the invitation, but underlying the thrill was a feeling of great disappointment. She had missed Tavia greatly during the past few months . . . but stronger than the desire to see her sister again was the desire to see Silvan. Though Jansie had tried to forget her longings, her efforts had been futile. She still dreamed of Silvan each night, still thought of him each day. And now, when the long-awaited invitation had finally come, he would not be there. It seemed a bitterly cruel blow.

But if she would not see Silvan himself, she thought, at least she would see his house, and that prospect fascinated her. So the following day she set out with Gilmer as escort.

The morning was bright but cold, with frost glittering on the hedgerows and a fresh, chill snap to the wind. The ponies' hoofs rang and echoed cheerfully on the road, and as they trotted along, Jansie looked sidelong at her companion. Gilmer had a charming

manner, she thought. Handsome, too –
though in a very different way from
Silvan, for Gilmer was smaller, slim
without being gaunt, and had warm grey
eyes and thick, fair hair in which the
winter sun made rainbows of colour. He
was obviously attracted to Jansie, and
she knew that if circumstances had been
different she might well have been drawn
to him. But each time she looked at
Gilmer, the shadow of Silvan moved
across her inner vision. It was wrong,
Jansie *knew* it was wrong. But her
brother-in-law had snared her heart, and
she could have no thought for anyone
else.

They did talk a great deal on the
journey, however, and Jansie soon
learned that Gilmer was no ordinary
servant. He came from an old, respected
and once-wealthy family, but in recent
years they had fallen on hard times.
Gilmer knew a great deal about
herbalism and his ambition was to
become a physician. But such training

cost money, and so Gilmer now worked for Silvan, as his steward. Soon they were laughing and talking like old friends.

'Well, Jansie, I'm glad to hear you so cheerful despite the cold!' Gilmer dropped the reins for a moment and rubbed his hands together. 'Winter's early this year, and it looks set to be a bitter one. We even had a snowfall on the Winter Solstice, and that's very rare – in fact I don't think it's happened before in my father's lifetime, let alone in mine.'

'You mean you don't get snow?' Jansie was surprised.

'Oh yes, we do, but usually not until a month after the Solstice is past. The forest where we – that is, where your sister and brother-in-law live is very sheltered. Cool in the summer, warm in the winter. Only this year the weather seems to have something else in mind. A few days ago, I even heard –' Then, as though thinking better of it, he broke off abruptly.

Jansie looked at him, curious. 'What did you hear?'

'Oh, nothing.' But there was a strange expression on Gilmer's face. 'It isn't important.'

But it was. Jansie could tell. And as they rode on, suddenly silent, she felt a sense of creeping unease begin to form somewhere very deep in her mind . . .

Chapter Two

THE SUN WAS setting on the fourth day of their journey when at last they reached their destination. The ponies crested a ridge; suddenly before them was a great sweep of forest – and, dominating the scene from a hill on the forest's edge, stood Silvan's house.

Jansie stared at the house with a mixture of awe and dismay. It was very large, far larger than her own home, and in all her life she had never seen a building that looked so grim and gloomy. Grey stone walls reared up, crowned with towers and turrets, and the great, arched entrance was like a dark mouth waiting to devour them.

The ponies clattered under the arch and into a courtyard lit by torches. Gilmer helped Jansie to dismount and she gazed up at the narrow windows, wondering how Tavia could bear to live in such a place. But then, Tavia had Silvan . . .

As if her thought had cast some peculiar spell, Silvan himself emerged from the main door at that moment. Jansie's heart gave a painful lurch as the torches lit his high-boned face and the white streak of hair. Then she took a grip on herself and went forward to greet him. He kissed her – a brotherly kiss, and she *longed* for it to be more – and said, 'Jansie, I'm so glad you could make the journey. Come inside. Tavia is eager to see you.'

The great hall overlooked the courtyard and was a huge, imposing chamber filled with antiques and relics. A fire blazed in the vast hearth, keeping the worst of the shadows at bay, and a long, polished table was set ready for a meal.

Tavia jumped up from a chair by the fire and ran to her sister. 'Jansie! Oh, it's wonderful to see you!'

Jansie was shocked. Tavia had changed. At her wedding she had been vivid-eyed, rose-cheeked, beautiful, but now her face was pale and her body thin. She looked ill.

'Tavia, what's wrong?' Jansie asked. 'Have you had a fever?'

Tavia laughed, though there was a funny little edge to the laugh. 'A fever? Of course not – I'm perfectly well! Come along now, come to the fire and get warm.'

Silvan took Jansie's cloak, then Gilmer came in and, before long, they were all sitting down to a lavish meal. It was a cheerful enough affair, but Jansie couldn't shake off a feeling of unease that grew stronger as the evening progressed. And it wasn't just the house's atmosphere that troubled her, for she was sure now that something was wrong with Tavia. On the surface her sister seemed happy, but occasionally Jansie saw something else in her face, and the only name she could give that something was fear.

As for Silvan . . . he was in a strange mood, she thought. He seemed very restless. He kept looking towards the window, and twice he asked Gilmer if he thought it would snow again soon. He planned to leave on his journey in the morning, and Jansie had the impression that he was very anxious indeed to be away.

The meal ended, and Silvan said that, with an early start ahead of him tomorrow, he would retire to bed. Tavia went too, and when they were gone, Gilmer was about to leave when suddenly he paused.

'Jansie,' he asked hesitantly, 'is something wrong?'

Jansie was still sitting at the table, staring down at its polished surface. She made to shrug the question off, but abruptly changed her mind. If anything *was* amiss with her sister, then surely Gilmer might know and be able to explain? So she said, 'It's Tavia, Gilmer. She's so pale and thin – I'm worried about her.' She looked up, meeting his eyes. 'Please tell me the truth. Is she ill?'

Gilmer sighed. 'No,' he replied. 'Your sister isn't ill. But she is . . . troubled.'

Jansie frowned. 'What do you mean?'

'Well . . . it's just that she's started to have nightmares.'

'Nightmares?' Jansie was taken aback. 'What sort of nightmares?'

Gilmer shook his head. He looked uncomfortable. 'She hasn't told me. But she wakes up screaming sometimes, and Silvan's very worried.'

Little wonder, Jansie thought. Tavia had never had nightmares for as long as she could remember; it was one of the many things about her sister that Jansie envied.

'Well,' she said, 'perhaps she'll talk to me about it.'

Gilmer gave her an odd look. 'When Silvan has gone?'

Now what does that mean? Jansie wondered, but she didn't ask, only said, 'Yes. When he's gone.'

Jansie's room was large and richly furnished, with thick rugs, tapestries on the walls and a four-poster bed with crimson curtains. But for all its splendour, there was something very forbidding about it – just like the rest of this house, Jansie thought. With only Silvan, Tavia and a few servants living here, the house had an atmosphere of cold, brooding emptiness that seemed to chill her to the bone.

Lying in bed with the covers pulled up to her chin, Jansie stared at the flickering shadows cast by her candle flame and thought about the great hall downstairs.

It was full of heirlooms, some of them centuries old, for Silvan's family had a long history. One object in particular had sent a cold shiver through Jansie, but she couldn't say why. It was an ancient sword, made of bronze, which hung above the fireplace. There were gemstones set into the hilt, and something was written on the blade, though she hadn't looked closely enough to read the words. Silvan had said that it was the one thing he would never part with under any circumstances. There had been a peculiar note in his voice as he'd said it, and Tavia had looked quickly away.

Jansie shivered again. Sleep wouldn't come easily tonight, she was certain. The wind had risen now and was howling around the walls, rattling her window as though it were alive and had hands that were trying to pull the glass away. The house creaked, too, with a soft, groaning sound that made her think of a lamenting voice. Jansie stared at her candle and started to play a counting game in her mind, to distract her from the eerie sounds and the ominous atmosphere. She almost wished that she could go home tomorrow, ride away and never see this house again. But for Tavia's sake she would stay. She *must*.

Jansie did fall asleep at last, but her sleep was filled with strange dreams. Several times she woke with a start and was relieved to find the candle still burning. The shadows were unnerving, but darkness would be worse. And once, as she tried to settle to sleep again, she heard – or thought she did, she couldn't quite be sure – a new sound. It seemed to be coming from outside her room, in the corridor. Something *moving*. Something that shuffled, softly, slowly. And the shuffling was accompanied by a peculiar, rhythmic click . . .

Jansie tensed. She didn't dare go to investigate, but instead lay wide-eyed, listening. The sound seemed to pass her door, then it faded into nothing. Had she imagined it? Or was she still asleep and dreaming? She didn't know. But she was very, very frightened.

Then, in the darkest hour of the night, she was jolted awake again as a scream of terror rang through the house.

For a moment she was too shocked to move. But as the echoes of the scream died away, she suddenly realized where the cry had come from.

'Tavia!' Jansie sprang from the bed and ran out of the door towards her sister's room. The corridor was pitch dark and she took two wrong turns, but at last she found the room and burst in, calling Tavia's name.

Silvan and Gilmer were already there, and with them was one of the house-maids. They were all trying to calm Tavia as she rocked backwards and forwards in her bed, hands over her eyes, and sobbed hysterically. Horrified, Jansie ran to her. 'Tavia! What is it, what's happened?'

'It's another nightmare,' Gilmer said.

'The worst one yet.'

Silvan was bending over the bed. He had taken Tavia in his arms – Jansie hated herself for the stab of jealousy that went through her – and was trying to soothe her. But Tavia was too frightened to be soothed, and between sobs she was choking out words.

'The hound, the hound . . . oh, please, keep it away! Don't let it touch me!'

'Tavia –' Jansie started towards her sister, wanting to help though not knowing how. But suddenly she froze, and the hair at the nape of her neck rose with tingling horror.

For from outside in the night, far in the distance, but carried on the moaning wind, came the unearthly sound of dogs howling.

Silvan jerked upright, releasing Tavia and swinging round towards the window. Jansie saw his face – and for a moment, before he masked it, his expression was one of pure fear. Jansie's own fear was suddenly eclipsed by something else, and she started to say, 'Silvan, what's wrong?' But Silvan didn't hear – or didn't want to hear. Instead he turned quickly to Gilmer.

'Mix Tavia a calming potion!' he snapped. 'Quickly!'

Jansie had never heard him use such a tone before, and she watched him uncertainly, not daring to speak now, as he began to pace the room. Gilmer mixed a herbal drink and Tavia was persuaded to swallow it. Almost at once she began to calm down, and at last Silvan stopped pacing and returned to her side. The night was silent again but for the wind's voice; the howling had ceased. But Jansie felt as if spiders were crawling all over her skin.

'She'll sleep now,' Silvan said sharply. 'I'll stay with her; the rest of you can go back to bed.' With an effort he made himself look at Jansie. 'I'm sorry this has happened on your first night here.'

Jansie gazed back at him, at his stark face, and the longing that she always felt in his company was suddenly overshadowed by another, darker feeling. She couldn't bring herself to answer him, but only kissed her sister goodnight and followed Gilmer and the maid out of the door.

'I'll escort you back to your room,' Gilmer said. He was carrying a lantern, and by its light he smiled at her. 'You don't want to risk getting lost in the dark.'

They began to walk back along the corridor, and Jansie said, 'That howling –' She glanced sidelong at him. 'What *was* it, Gilmer? Wild dogs? Or wolves?'

Gilmer's face grew serious. 'Truthfully, I don't know,' he said. 'There have been rumours, but . . .' His voice tailed off.

Jansie began to feel very uneasy again. 'Rumours of what?'

'Well . . . there's an old legend about a pack of hounds that haunts this district.'

'Do you mean they're *ghosts*?'

'No one knows for sure,' said Gilmer.

'No one even knows if they really exist, and they haven't been heard of for many years. But this winter . . . it seems they've come back.' He shuddered. 'I heard them myself, on the night of the Winter Solstice. And some people in the village five miles away claim to have seen them.'

'*Seen* them?' Jansie echoed, appalled. 'Where?'

'In the forest, at night. A dozen or more, they say, all of them pure white except for their leader, which is jet-black. They call them the Hounds of Winter.'

The name made Jansie's skin prickle all over again. 'Are they dangerous?' she asked.

'Again, no one knows for sure. But five days ago a shepherd found three of his sheep dead in the pasture. Their throats had been torn out.'

Ghosts that could attack and kill . . .? An ice-cold feeling seemed to lodge in the pit of Jansie's stomach.

'Silvan could probably tell you more about the hounds than I can,' Gilmer added. 'His family have lived here for centuries.' He paused. 'But I don't think it would be a good idea to ask him.'

Jansie stopped walking. 'Why not?'

In the lantern light Gilmer's face looked strange suddenly and a new shadow seemed to fall across it. 'Because . . .' he said, 'I just don't think it would.'

Chapter Three

As if the events of the night weren't enough, the following morning brought a new surprise – for a blizzard was raging. Snow was already lying several feet deep in places, and the outside world was blotted out by a whirling storm of white.

The house was bitterly cold, and Jansie put on her warmest clothes before venturing downstairs. A servant said that Mistress Tavia was still sleeping; Master Silvan was somewhere about, but it would be as well to keep out of his way as he was in a very strange mood. He had had to put off his journey, the servant added, because the snow was already too deep for travelling. And he was not at all happy about it.

But if Silvan wasn't happy, Jansie was. For all the terrors of the night, it seemed that fate had smiled on her, and she ran at once to the great hall, hoping to find Silvan there. The hall was empty though, and, disappointed, she crossed to the window where she rubbed the condensation on the glass with her fist and tried to peer out.

The glass was rough under her hand . . . and, suddenly, as the moisture cleared, Jansie saw that something had been scratched on the window-pane. She looked closer. Crudely but clearly etched on the glass were five stark words.

HELP TAVIA. HELP US ALL.

Jansie's blood seemed to slow to a crawl as she stared at the scratched writing. *Who had done this? And why?*

Behind her the door closed, and, with a little cry of shock, she spun round.

Gilmer had come in. He stopped when he saw her, then his eyes narrowed as he took in the expression on her face. Jansie beckoned frantically.

'Gilmer, come here – look at this!'

He approached, and Jansie pointed to the glass. 'Look!' she said again.

Gilmer stared at the writing and uttered a soft oath.

'Gilmer, who could have written such a message?' Jansie's voice was fearful. 'What does it *mean*?'

'I don't know,' Gilmer replied. 'But one thing I'm sure of – it wasn't there last night.'

'What?'

'I looked out of this very window just before we sat down to dinner. If it had been there then, I would have seen it.' He paused. 'And what made the marks? It almost looks like . . . claws.'

Memories of the dogs howling in the night came sharply back to Jansie and she shrank from the window, half fearing that she might at any moment glimpse a lean, fanged face glaring in at her through the flying snow.

'The hounds . . .' she whispered.

'How could an animal make such marks?' Gilmer said softly. 'Unless . . .'

'Unless what?'

He turned to gaze at her. 'Unless these are no normal creatures. Maybe the legend of the Hounds of Winter is true . . .'

Gilmer asked Jansie to say nothing to Silvan about the ominous writing on the window. It would only worry him further, Gilmer said, and he had troubles enough at the moment.

It seemed Gilmer was right, for Silvan was in a strange, restless mood that day. He spent the entire morning pacing through the house like a caged animal before finally saying that he had work to do, shutting himself away in one of the tower rooms. Jansie's heart ached as she watched him leave. She had tried so hard to talk to him and cheer him, hoping that he would find some pleasure in her company. But though Silvan was pleasant to her, there was a remoteness, almost an iciness, behind his politeness. He was uninterested, like stone.

Tavia spent the morning in bed, and when she finally came downstairs, she was very withdrawn. She seemed relieved to know that Silvan was still at home, but when Jansie tried gently to probe into what might be wrong, Tavia wouldn't answer and changed the subject.

And that, it seemed, was how matters were destined to stay. The blizzard continued for two more nights, during which time the atmosphere in the house grew gloomier and more oppressive. Silvan still spent many hours in the tower, and on the few occasions when he did emerge, he was as withdrawn as Tavia, having few words to say to anyone. At mealtimes Jansie watched him furtively, yearning to break the silence, to *talk* to him. But she couldn't find the courage. And the fact that Tavia was sitting at his side made matters worse, for Jansie's conscience was being torn apart. How could she claim to love her sister and yet at the same time be in love with her sister's husband? Even by feeling the way she did, she thought, she was betraying Tavia's trust.

And while Jansie wistfully watched Silvan, Gilmer wistfully watched Jansie. He knew very well how Jansie felt about Silvan. Her infatuation was in every look she gave him, every movement she made towards him. And, though he tried to deny it, Gilmer was miserably jealous.

Yet Gilmer also knew that Silvan did not love Jansie as she loved him. That gave him at least a little hope, and he clung to that hope, thinking that perhaps as Jansie grew to know him better, her feelings might change.

Jansie knew very well what was in Gilmer's mind and heart. And she had to admit to herself that she did like him. But although they were becoming friends, Gilmer was nothing more to her. The shadow of Silvan, haunting her mind by day and night, made anything else impossible.

Two more days passed. The blizzard had at last abated, but snow was still falling and the world was completely blanketed in white so that no one could travel. Jansie's nights were still very troubled. Each evening when she went to bed, she lay awake for a long time listening to the house's creaking, which never seemed to cease. To her vivid and nervous imagination it sounded as if the house was breathing, slowly, like a huge, sinister and dangerous animal that might wake at any moment. And it gave a chilly, uneasy edge to her unhappy longings about Silvan, so that when she finally fell asleep, her dreams of him were filled with fear.

On the fourth night, a little after midnight, she was dreaming that the house *had* come to life, and that she and Silvan were trying desperately to get out before it devoured them, when suddenly she started awake.

The awful breathing-creaking had stopped. Instead, an eerie, wailing cry shivered in the silence of the night.

The hounds . . . Jansie jolted upright, hugging herself. It sounded as if they were horrifyingly close by, and she was trying to pluck up the courage to get out of bed and tiptoe to the window, when something else made her pause. Not out there in the snow, but in the house. A shuffling. The same noise she had heard before, and again it was coming from the passage outside her room. But this time there was more.

The sound of someone breathing . . .

Very slowly, Jansie turned her head and looked at the bedroom door. She couldn't be sure, but it seemed that a shadow moved in the gap between the bottom of the door and the floorboards. She wanted to call out, ask who was there, but when she tried to speak, her throat wouldn't make a sound.

Then the door creaked and began to swing open.

A strange, cold light shone in from the corridor, like the eerie glow of snow under the moon. And framed in the doorway was a black dog.

Jansie's heart stopped beating. The dog was *huge*, far bigger than any normal animal. Its fur was long, flowing over its back like dark silk. But all along its spine the hackles were raised, and its head was menacingly lowered . . . and its eyes glared with an insane light.

Then the dog opened its mouth and a soft, foreboding growl rumbled in its throat. Long, yellow fangs glinted in the light, and its mouth slavered. The head dropped further, the powerful hindquarters tensed – and it sprang.

Jansie flung herself sideways as the dark shape arrowed towards her in a wild, flying leap. She heard her own voice shriek in shrill terror, and then the

black dog's weight crashed on to the
bed, on to her, and she was fighting for
her life, screaming for help as her hands
flailed frantically in an attempt to keep
off the snapping teeth and scrabbling
claws. The dog's snarls and her own
cries dinned in her ears. She could feel
its hot breath on her face; it was going to
savage her, it was going to *kill* her –

'*Jansie!*' In the mayhem she hadn't
heard the running footsteps in the
corridor, but suddenly Gilmer burst into
the room with two servants behind him.
Growling, the hound spun round. It saw
them – with one movement its powerful
body twisted and it leaped from the bed,
hurling itself straight at the window.
There was a shattering noise as the
window smashed, flinging fragments of
glass in all directions like an explosion,
and the great dog hurtled through and
out into the night.

'Jansie!' Gilmer rushed to her side as
the servants ran to the window. 'Jansie,
Jansie, are you hurt?'

Jansie clung to him, gasping like someone rescued at the last moment from drowning. 'Gilmer, oh, Gilmer!' Her hands clutched his arms and she thought she was going to faint. 'It came in, and it was so hideous, and it –'

'Hush, now, hush!' Gilmer hugged her. 'It's gone now and you're safe! Oh, Jansie, if anything had happened to you . . .' Then he cut the words off, knowing he dared not say them.

There was a sudden new commotion outside and more servants came in. They were horrified when they heard the story. How could the creature have got into the house? No ordinary animal could have entered, they said – this was something supernatural, a demon-dog, a monster!

In the midst of this excited babble, Tavia and her maid arrived, and when Tavia heard what the servants were saying, she was furious. There were no such things as demon-dogs, she snapped angrily, and her sister had already been frightened badly enough without such gossip to make matters worse! Whatever attacked Jansie had been a wild animal of flesh and blood. Now, the men must search the house and grounds to see if they could find out where it had come from and where it might have gone. In the mean time, Jansie would be given another bedroom, and a servant would be set to guard the corridor for the rest of the night to keep everyone safe.

Gilmer and Tavia led the still-shivering Jansie along the passage to another hastily prepared bedroom. She kept glancing back over her shoulder, and though Tavia thought she was afraid of seeing the dog again, Gilmer knew better. Jansie was looking for Silvan. Still up in his tower, he either had not heard the disturbance or had chosen to ignore it. Jansie was hurt and disappointed. Was Silvan so indifferent to her? She couldn't understand why he had not come to ensure that she was safe.

And neither could Gilmer . . .

In the new room Jansie was settled in bed and Gilmer gave her a herbal potion to help her sleep. As he left, he looked back with sad wistfulness, but said nothing. The door closed behind him, and quickly Tavia turned to her sister.

'Jansie!' Her voice was soft and urgent. Jansie was already drowsy from the potion, but she opened her eyes.

'Jansie, listen to me!' Tavia said. 'Don't tell anyone I said this – whatever you do, don't tell *anyone*! But as soon as it's possible to travel again, you must go home. For your own sake and mine, you *mustn't* stay here!'

Jansie's mind was fuddled and she didn't understand. What did Tavia mean? But before she could even begin to ask, Tavia had hurried across the room and opened the door. She paused, seemed about to say something else, then changed her mind and ran from the room as though something dark and dreadful were pursuing her.

Chapter Four

THE SERVANTS FOUND no trace of the black hound. By the time they reached the courtyard, the falling snow had blotted out any prints the creature might have left, and though they searched for two hours the dog had vanished into thin air.

All day there was a tense atmosphere in the house. The snow had stopped falling but a gloomy, iron-hard cold had clamped down on the world. Jansie spent the afternoon in the kitchen, which seemed to be the only warm room, helping Gilmer to sort some dried herbs, then went up to her chilly bedroom to change her dress for dinner.

Coming downstairs again and approaching the great hall, Jansie suddenly paused. The doors were closed, but from the other side she could hear raised voices. Silvan and Tavia – and it sounded as if they were quarrelling.

Jansie knew she shouldn't eavesdrop, but the temptation was too great to resist. Silvan was speaking; he seemed to be pleading with Tavia, but the heavy wooden doors muffled the sound of his voice and made it impossible to hear what he was saying. But then Tavia's voice went up shrilly and clearly.

'No!' she cried. 'No, no, NO! I won't do it! Not even for your sake – I *can't*!'

Jansie tensed. Whatever was going on? What was it that Tavia 'couldn't' do? Silvan was replying now, angrily, though again she was unable to make out his words. Then came a violent clattering sound, making Jansie jump, and Silvan shouted, 'Don't you understand? The snow's come and that means it's too late to change anything! It's got to be done!'

Tavia whimpered. Then the clattering sounded again, and suddenly her voice rose to a scream. 'No, Silvan! I won't touch it, I won't even *look* at it!'

Horrified by the terror in her sister's voice, Jansie couldn't stop herself; she flung the door open and rushed into the room.

Tavia and Silvan were standing in front of the fireplace. Silvan had taken down the ancient sword from above the mantel and was holding it out towards Tavia. But she had turned her back on him. She had covered her face with both hands and was cowering from her husband.

Or, Jansie thought, from the sword . . .

Then Silvan saw Jansie. For an instant his face twisted into a furious expression, then with a tremendous effort he brought himself under control.

'Jansie . . .' He lowered the sword and stared at her. 'We . . . didn't hear you come in.'

Tavia's head came up sharply. There were tears on her cheeks and she wiped them quickly away. Jansie said uneasily, 'I heard shouting . . .'

'Shouting?' Tavia sniffed, then gave a strange little laugh. 'We weren't shouting. Were we, Silvan? No, no; it was just a – a little misunderstanding. Nothing important.'

'No,' Silvan echoed. 'Nothing important at all.'

'Well.' Tavia smoothed her hair. She wouldn't meet Jansie's eyes. 'Gilmer will be here in a moment and then we can all eat. Here, Jansie, come and sit down.'

They were both lying. Jansie knew it, and they knew that she knew. But there was nothing she could say. Their quarrels were none of her business and she had no right to interfere. But she watched Silvan as he put the sword back in its place over the hearth. His hands were shaking and his face wore an expression that sent a shiver through her. Silvan was very, very angry. But there was something else in his look, far stronger than the anger. It was the same expression that he had shown when Tavia had her nightmare and the dogs had howled outside in the night. Silvan was afraid.

Dinner that evening was eaten in uneasy silence. Silvan seemed anxious that the snow continued to prevent his departure. He and Tavia had nothing to say to each other or anyone else, and Jansie and Gilmer both felt too uncomfortable to talk. No one wanted to eat much, and they were all thankful when at last the old servant cleared the dishes away. As soon as he had gone, Tavia rose from the table.

'I'm very tired,' she said stiffly. 'I think I shall go to bed.' She gave a quick, almost furtive glance around and forced a smile. 'Goodnight.'

Tavia's departure seemed to act as a signal for the rest of them to go their separate ways. Silvan said that he was going to the tower to work on his papers. Gilmer had some studying to do. And so Jansie was left alone in the hall.

For several minutes she sat at the table, listening to the crackle of the fire and the more ominous noise of the wind outside. She couldn't stop thinking about what she had overheard, and her gaze strayed uneasily towards the sword hanging in its place above the hearth. She suppressed a shiver. There was something strange about that ancient weapon. Tavia was obviously terrified of even touching it, yet Silvan had been trying to make her take it from him. What dark mystery was at work here?

Jansie recalled all the small incidents that had happened since her arrival. Tavia's nightmare. The howling dogs. The chilling message scratched on the window-pane. The creature that had got into the house and tried to attack her. And her sister's cryptic warning . . .

Then abruptly Jansie remembered the

words she had glimpsed on the blade on her first evening. She hadn't dared to look more closely then, and a part of her didn't want to look now. But another – and stronger – part felt a strange compulsion to know what was written there. And she was alone in the room now. No one need find out . . .

Quickly, before her courage could fail her, Jansie crossed to the fireplace and climbed on to a stool. The sword was very heavy, but she managed to lift it down and carried it back to the table. A draught made the candles flicker as she set the sword down, and shadows loomed suddenly, making her start with nerves. Ignoring this feeling – shadows couldn't hurt her, after all – she bent over the blade.

There, in a strange, old-fashioned script, were the words:

I was your salvation.
And I shall be your doom.

Jansie stared at the dully gleaming sword. Such ominous words. What could they, possibly *mean*?

A sudden noise made her jump violently. She spun round. The door had opened and Tavia stood on the threshold. She was in her nightgown, and for a moment she stared at Jansie as though she were a stranger. Then she saw the sword and said, 'Ah . . .'

Jansie's cheeks flamed scarlet. 'Tavia, I wasn't meddling!' she protested desperately. 'I only –'

Tavia interrupted her. 'It doesn't matter,' she said in a flat voice. 'Nothing matters any more.' Another glance at the sword, and she shuddered. 'Is Silvan in the tower?'

'Yes,' said Jansie.

Tavia nodded. 'Very well. That was all I wanted to know.' She turned round, then looked over her shoulder. 'Put the sword back. I . . . do not wish it to be taken down again.' She paused. 'I know what the words say. And I don't want

46

them to come true.' Another pause. 'Be careful, Jansie. Please – be careful.'

And with that she went out and closed the door.

Jansie stood very still until Tavia's footsteps had faded into silence. What had her sister meant, 'be careful'? What did Tavia think was going to happen?

She carried the sword to the fireplace and put it back in its place. In the dying firelight it seemed to glow with a grim life of its own. For a few moments longer Jansie stood gazing at it. Then, very softly, she tiptoed out and away to her room.

Jansie tried to make sense of her thoughts, but it was impossible. All she had to guide her was the feeling that some nameless peril hung over the house and everyone in it. At last she gave up her efforts. It must be past midnight; she should try to sleep.

The house was very quiet, but just as Jansie settled down under her blankets, there was a sudden flurry of running footsteps along the corridor and the sound of someone calling out. Puzzled, Jansie got out of bed and opened her door to look out.

One of the maids was on the landing. 'Miss Jansie!' she cried breathlessly. 'Oh, please come quickly!'

Jansie's spine prickled. 'What is it? What's happened?'

'It's Mistress Tavia!' The maid was tearful, close to panic. 'I went to her room just moments ago, to make up the fire and see if there was anything she wanted. But she wasn't there. I thought perhaps she was with Master Silvan, or with you. But then I saw that her cloak and shoes had gone, and so had her valise.' The girl drew breath. 'Oh, miss – I think the mistress has run away!'

Chapter Five

GILMER ORDERED THE servants to start a search while he went to the tower to alert Silvan. Within minutes the house was in turmoil, but they found nothing. At last they were forced to face the truth – that, as the maid feared, Tavia had gone.

But when Silvan and Gilmer, carrying lanterns, went out into the bitter night, they found the first tell-tale sign. A small side door in the house was standing open, and new footprints led from this door and away towards the forest.

'The forest?' Jansie put her hands to her mouth in horror when Gilmer told her. 'Oh, no! The danger – she'll freeze to death! Or –' She stopped and her eyes widened.

'Gilmer.' In the hall's flickering candlelight Silvan's face looked stark, almost dangerous. 'I want every man ready in five minutes with a lantern. We'll follow Tavia's footprints as far as we can and then spread out and search the forest.'

'You're going after her now?' Jansie asked in alarm.

'Of course.' Silvan gave her a strange, angry look and she felt ashamed. He was right; they must go immediately.

'Please,' she said in a small voice, gazing at him. 'Be careful . . .'

Gilmer looked away, wishing that her concern was for him, and Silvan uttered a peculiar, harsh laugh. 'Don't fret, Jansie,' he said, and there was a bitter edge to his voice. 'I won't come to any harm.'

*

Through the night Jansie waited anxiously for news. In the deep snow Tavia couldn't have got far, but the snow would hamper the searchers too. As she paced up and down the hall, Jansie's blood was running cold with fear for her sister.

Why had Tavia run away? That was what Jansie couldn't understand. She must have known the danger – what could have made her so desperate that she would risk her life rather than stay here? What was she so afraid of?

Or, Jansie thought, her skin crawling, *who* was she so afraid of?

Shadows seemed to gather around her as the answer to that question crept into her mind. She didn't want to acknowledge it, but it gnawed at her, sending a feeling like icy fingers down her spine. Tavia was afraid of Silvan. And the mystery that surrounded them both had something to do with that ancient bronze sword.

She glanced towards the fireplace,

where the sword hung in its bracket above the hearth. For a moment she was tempted to lift it down again and examine it more closely, but with an inward shiver she thought better of it. She didn't want to touch the sword again. Like Tavia, she was afraid of it.

Outside the wind seemed to laugh at Jansie's terrors. And carried on the wind, faint and distant, she imagined she could hear the sound of dogs howling . . .

The searchers started to return an hour before dawn. Gilmer was with the first party to arrive; Jansie ran to the front door to meet him, and the expression on his face told her the news instantly. They had found nothing. They had pressed on as far as they could into the forest, but there was not the slightest trace of Tavia.

Before long all the searchers were back . . . except for Silvan. They had lost sight of him some time ago, Gilmer said, but he reassured Jansie that Silvan would be safe. He knew the forest better than any of them. He would come to no harm.

Jansie wished she could believe that, but as the minutes passed and still Silvan didn't appear, her terror deepened. It was snowing again, and to her fevered imagination that made the danger worse. What if Silvan didn't come back? What if both he and Tavia met the spectral hounds out there in the night?

But at last the glimmer of a lantern appeared in the distance, and Silvan arrived. He was exhausted, hollow-eyed and stumbling, and starkly he told them that he, too, had found nothing.

There was a flurry of activity then as hot food and drinks were prepared and everyone gathered their strength for a new search. This time Jansie was determined to go with them, and though both Silvan and Gilmer argued against it, she was adamant.

★

They searched all through the morning. The snow had stopped again, but the sky was dreary grey and the day bitterly cold. It was as if, Jansie thought with a shudder, the whole world had been sealed into a lead coffin from which there was no hope of escape.

The forest was utterly silent. No birds sang, nothing moved, and in the green-tinged gloom the pine trees crowded round them like sinister phantoms. Gilmer stayed close to Jansie. She was grateful for his company, yet she wished that it was Silvan walking at her side instead. Now and then she glimpsed Silvan some distance ahead of them. His dark figure seemed to blend with the trees, so that he looked like a ghost himself, and each time she saw him, Jansie felt the twin pangs of guilt and yearning strike her yet again. She loved him so much. And – especially now, with Tavia missing – her love was so very, very wrong.

It was nearly noon when the search ended. Jansie and Gilmer were struggling through a deep patch of snow when a shout rang out from a nearby clearing.

'Here! Here, quickly!'

Jansie's heart lurched with sick fear as they hurried towards the sound. Gilmer reached the clearing before her; as she ran up to him, he turned and caught hold of her arms, trying to stop her.

'No, Jansie, wait!' he said. 'It's better that you don't –'

But Jansie had already pushed past him. Three men were gathered round something dark that lay at the edge of the clearing. For a moment it looked like a fallen tree half buried in the snow. But then she saw that the darkness was not tree bark, but a cloak. Above the cloak was a glint of golden hair. And the snow all around was stained crimson.

'Tavia . . .?' Fear and disbelief filled Jansie's voice as she stared down at the still form of her sister. For just an instant it seemed to her that Tavia was simply asleep, for her eyes were closed and her face, though deathly white, looked peaceful. But then Jansie saw her throat beneath the pale cheeks. She saw what the dogs had done to her.

'Oh, no . . .' Fear turned to horror, and Jansie's voice rose in a shrill scream that echoed through the forest. 'Oh, no, *no*, NO! *TAVIA!!*'

Gilmer caught her as she reeled back, and she clung to him, hiding her face against his shoulder and sobbing wildly. He held her close, desperately trying to find words, but knowing that nothing he could say would be of any use. Then new footfalls crunched in the snow, and he looked round.

Silvan had arrived. He stopped when he saw Tavia's body, and as he stared at her, his hands began to shake. He said nothing. He made no sound. But all the colour drained from his skin and his eyes grew as hard as steel. Then, suddenly, he turned away and covered his face. And as Gilmer stood helpless with Jansie in his arms, he heard Silvan weeping.

Chapter Six

THE SNOW STILL made it impossible to travel any great distance, and so they couldn't even send a message breaking the terrible news to Jansie's parents. Nor could Jansie herself return home. And that was her only crumb of comfort in a world that had suddenly turned to black misery.

For two days, while preparations were made for Tavia's funeral, Jansie lay in her room. Thanks to Gilmer's potions, she slept for most of the time, but whenever she did wake, she could do nothing but cry.

At last, though, the worst of the shock passed and she was able to get up. The house was gloomy and uncannily quiet. All the curtains had been drawn as a sign of mourning, and no lamps were lit. The servants moved softly, not speaking, their faces sad and haunted.

And Silvan was like a man who had turned to stone.

Then, in the deep silence of the night before the funeral, Jansie woke to find a strange light shining in her room.

For a moment she thought it must be the glow of her fire. But this light was almost colourless, and it did not flicker as flames did but shone steadily, like moonlight. Jansie sat up in bed, staring, and saw that a pale oval had taken form in the middle of the room, seeming to hang suspended in mid-air.

Then, within the oval, a figure began to appear.

Jansie's eyes opened with fear as the figure took shape. For a moment she was on the verge of screaming. But then she saw that the figure was that of a girl. And the girl had blue eyes, and long blonde hair . . .

Jansie's heart seemed to stop beating, and in a soft, stunned voice she whispered:

'*Tavia?*'

From the glowing oval of light, Tavia gazed back at her. She was wearing a long white gown – a funeral gown, Jansie realized with a jolt of horror – and her face was so sad that tears started into Jansie's eyes.

'Oh, Tavia,' she quavered. 'Tavia, is it really you . . .?'

Tavia nodded, and an odd little sound, like an unhappy sigh, breathed through the room. Then she spoke. It was like listening to a voice in a dream, faraway and echoey. But Jansie heard her words clearly.

'*Ah, Jansie,*' Tavia said. '*I could not do

what must be done. I did not love him enough. But you do, Jansie. You do.'

She gave another sigh, and her image began to fade from the oval of light.

'Tavia!' Jansie cried in distress. 'Tavia, what do you mean? I don't understand!'

Tavia gazed wistfully at her. '*After tomorrow, it will be too late for me,'* her eerie voice said. '*But it is not yet too late for you. You can save us, Jansie. You can save us all . . .'*

The oval was dimming. Tavia was vanishing away. And seconds later Jansie sat staring helplessly at a dark and empty room.

She told no one of her strange experience; not Gilmer, and certainly not Silvan. Had it been a dream? Or had Tavia's ghost truly appeared to her? Jansie didn't know, and neither could she even begin to understand Tavia's strange words. *You can save us all.* But how could she save Tavia now? Jansie asked herself miserably. She had already failed to help her sister, and now it was far too late.

The dream – or whatever it had been – continued to haunt her as, with a heavy heart, she prepared for the funeral. The day was bleak and grey and icy, and frost glittered in the bare courtyard as the sad procession left the house and began the slow, mournful walk to Silvan's family vault in the grounds. Jansie started to shiver as they approached the grim, grey structure. For centuries Silvan's ancestors had been entombed here in their stone coffins, and now his wife was coming to join them. They entered the vault, and Jansie shivered again as the ominous atmosphere of gloom and cobwebs closed around her.

A priest had come from the village to perform the ceremony, but there were no flowers for Tavia, and no speeches. Silvan wanted it that way. Jansie's heart ached for her brother-in-law as she watched him. He stood motionless throughout the service, his face bleak. It was as if, she thought, he too was dead . . . or wished he was.

Nor was there a funeral feast afterwards. The priest and a few villagers who had come to pay their respects simply went home. As the door of the vault closed with a hollow and final *clang*, Silvan turned and, without so much as looking at anyone, stalked back towards the house. Gilmer, Jansie and the servants followed more slowly. No one spoke, for no one could think of anything to say. They reached the unlit house and found Silvan in the entrance hall. In the gloom he looked like a ghost himself, and Jansie wished with all her heart that she could offer him some comfort. But there was no comfort she could give.

Heavy snow began to fall again that night. Gilmer saw it through the window as he sat alone in the kitchen. Everyone else had gone to bed, but although he was tired, Gilmer didn't feel like sleeping. His heart was leaden, for he could not stop thinking about Jansie . . . and Silvan. With Tavia gone, Silvan was a single man again. For a long time yet he would have no interest in another woman. But time would heal the wound eventually. And in a year or two, Jansie would be old enough to think of marriage . . .

Gilmer sighed. He knew that Jansie already harboured hopes of one day becoming Silvan's wife. But Gilmer feared that if Silvan, in his turn, should ever fall in love with Jansie, she would be in terrible danger.

He got up and paced about the room, angry with himself. He had no right to think such things! Silvan was not a threat to Jansie – he was only a threat to Gilmer's own dreams.

The trouble is, Gilmer thought to himself, *I'm jealous. Jealous because Silvan is wealthy and handsome, and because Jansie is too enraptured with him ever to look twice at me.*

There was no point in sitting up any longer; his thoughts would only depress him more. Taking a candle, Gilmer went through the dark house and up the stairs towards his room.

And then, as he neared his door, a faint sound behind him made him stop . . .

Gilmer swung round. A shadow was moving at the end of the landing, heading towards the stairs. A long shadow, very sleek. And, faintly, Gilmer heard what sounded like the click of an animal's claws on the floor.

Quickly Gilmer snuffed out the candle and peered harder. And as the shadow reached the top of the staircase, the snowlight coming in at the window fell upon it.

It was a hound. A huge hound, gaunt and menacing, moving stealthily on to the stairs. Its fur was as black as a starless night – but for a single, long streak of pure white that ran from the top of its head and down the length of its back.

Gilmer's heart started to pound in his chest, for he realized that this monstrous creature had come from the direction of the tower room where Silvan spent so many hours. And with a sense of crawling horror he remembered that Silvan, too, had a single streak of white in his black hair . . .

On the stairs the hound merged with the shadows and disappeared. Should he call for help? Gilmer asked himself. One shout would bring the servants running. Yet if they came, the hound would surely flee. It would be better to follow it himself and see where it was going.

Very slowly and cautiously, Gilmer started to move along the landing. Reaching the top of the stairs he paused, listening. There was no sound. He began to creep down the stairs, but by the time he reached the hall, the hound was nowhere to be seen.

Frustration seethed in him. Where was the creature? It couldn't have vanished, and Gilmer began to wonder if he had dreamed or imagined it.

There seemed nothing for it but to go to bed. In the morning he would investigate and look for any tell-tale signs of the animal's presence. But for now there was no more he could do. The hound would not be sighted again tonight.

Or so he thought . . .

Jansie couldn't sleep, and was sitting by her window looking out at the courtyard. She was still worrying over the mystery of the ancient sword when suddenly a movement outside in the snowy night alerted her. The front door of the house was swinging open . . .

Jansie's eyes widened in shock as a dark, lean shape emerged from the house. It was the black hound! For a horrifying moment she thought it would look up and see her, but instead it paced over to the steps and stood still, gazing out at the night. Then, with a sound that made Jansie's spine prickle, it raised its head and gave voice to a soft, haunting cry.

For perhaps another minute all was still. But then, dimly though the whirling snow, Jansie glimpsed pale shapes moving towards the house. Closer and closer they came, running fast, until suddenly they loomed out of the murk and she saw them clearly. A pack of dogs, white and spectral and strange. The Hounds of Winter – and they were answering the summons of their leader.

Jansie hardly dared to breathe as she stared down at the courtyard. The white dogs gathered around the steps in a half-circle. They all gazed at their leader, as though waiting for some new sign. But the black hound was intent on something else. It gazed across the garden, towards the gloomy grey vault where the funeral had taken place. And from the vault, another white dog was approaching.

It came slowly, hesitantly, as if afraid. But the leader gave a small, sharp yip and an unseen power seemed to compel the newcomer forward. It joined the others, its head hanging low as if in defeat. And then, chilling Jansie to the bone, the dogs all raised their heads as one, and a long, desolate cry rang out through the night.

The black hound bounded down the steps. His pack parted to let him through and he sprang away across the courtyard, towards the garden and the forest beyond. Like water flowing, all the others turned and streaked after him – all but the last dog, the newcomer, which turned and looked straight up at Jansie's window.

Jansie realized that the dog had seen her, but to her astonishment it didn't snarl and threaten. Instead, it raised one paw as though trying to reach her. Trying, she thought, to *plead*.

Suddenly Jansie no longer felt afraid. The black hound had vanished – this was something different. She opened the window and leaned out. 'What are you?' she said. 'What do you want with me?'

The white hound whimpered. Then it ran to the ground-floor window directly below hers, and Jansie heard a scratching sound. What was it doing? Trying to get in? But no; for now the dog had moved back. It gazed up at her for one more moment, and then with swift grace it turned and raced away after the rest of the pack.

Jansie stared until it disappeared into the snow. What had it done? What had it been trying to tell her? She *had* to know! Snatching up a candle, she hurried out on to the landing and crept downstairs. Which room was directly below her own? At first she couldn't remember, but at last she found the right door. It was a store-room that wasn't often used. The chamber was dusty and the windows grey with cobwebs, but Jansie pushed them aside and held her candle up to the glass.

The white hound had scratched something on the window-pane. And as she looked at the shaky letters, Jansie felt dread take hold of her with a steel grip.

There were only three words. They read: 'I WAS TAVIA'.

Chapter Seven

BY THE TIME morning broke, Jansie had hardly slept – and she was frightened.

She wanted to believe that what she had seen last night was a dream, but she could not. For soon after daybreak she had returned to the store-room, and the scratchings on the glass were still there.

I WAS TAVIA. The words sent a spear of ice through Jansie each time she thought about them. The Hounds of Winter had killed her sister – and now it seemed that poor, unhappy Tavia had been transformed into one of them and was doomed to run with the pack! The idea was horrifying, and Jansie's first instinct had been to tell Gilmer. But Gilmer would surely insist on telling Silvan, and Jansie didn't want that. Silvan had already suffered enough, she thought. For now, at least, it would be better to investigate alone and see what she could discover. And the best way to look for answers was among Tavia's belongings.

She waited until the servants were in another part of the house, then made her way to her sister's room. At Silvan's orders it hadn't been touched since Tavia's death, and the sight of her clothes, the unmade bed, the uncleared fireplace, made Jansie shiver. Everything looked so *normal*. She could almost believe that at any moment Tavia would walk in and everything would be as it was before.

Pushing the thought away, she began to search. Slippers by the hearth, clothes in the wardrobe; nothing here to give her any clues. On the bedside table was a book Tavia had been reading, and on the window-ledge were more books in a neat pile. Jansie was about to pass them by when she saw that one of the volumes was sticking out from the rest. As if there was something else behind it . . .

She pulled the book out. Another, much smaller book slipped from where it had been hidden and fell to the floor.

Jansie picked it up. It had a plain brown cover with no lettering on it, and was fastened with a locked clasp. She felt a lurch of excitement, for she realized at once what it was. Tavia's diary . . .

Jansie's pulse began to race. There was no key; did she dare break the clasp and look at what the diary contained? For here, she was certain, must lie the truth about Tavia and what she had become.

Suddenly she heard footsteps in the passage, and the chattering voices of two maids. Quickly Jansie pushed the diary into the wide sleeve of her dress, then she slipped out of the room before she could be discovered. Back in her bedchamber she sat down and tried to make a decision. The idea of prying into Tavia's secrets made her very uncomfortable – but surely her sister would understand? Surely it was what she *wanted*?

She was still debating with herself when there was a knock at the door.

'Jansie?' It was Gilmer's voice. 'Jansie, may I come in?'

Jansie thrust the diary out of sight. 'Yes,' she called.

The door opened and Gilmer entered. He looked unhappy, and he said, 'Jansie, I have to talk to you. It's about . . . it's about the Hounds.'

Gilmer, too, had been in turmoil all morning. At first he intended to say nothing about his eerie experience with the black hound. But finally he had decided that it was wrong to hide it from

Jansie. She had to know the truth – it was only fair.

Jansie listened as he told her what he had seen the night before. When he finished, her face was sombre.

'Oh, Gilmer,' she said softly. 'Something happened to me too.' As he spoke she had realized that she couldn't keep her own story to herself any longer. She desperately needed to tell someone. And she could surely trust Gilmer to keep the secret.

She stood up. 'Come downstairs,' she said. 'There's something I must show you.'

She took him to the store-room and pointed to the window. And she described all that she had seen: the hound emerging from the house, the white dogs coming at their leader's call – and the last dog, arriving from the direction of the vault and scratching its chilling message on the glass.

'And, Gilmer, there's something more,' she added. 'Something that happened on the night before the funeral . . .'

She related the tale of Tavia's ghostly visit. When she finished, the expression on Gilmer's face was very grim, and Jansie's eyes narrowed abruptly. 'Gilmer?' she said uneasily. 'What is it?' Then intuition flared in her mind. 'You know something else, don't you? Something you haven't told me.'

Gilmer did. One small thing that he had left out of his own story. He had thought it better not to reveal to Jansie. Now, though . . .

'Jansie . . .' His voice was a little unsteady. 'I didn't want to say this to you, but I think I must. It's about the black hound, and – and Silvan.'

'Silvan?' She stared at him.

'Yes. When I saw the hound last night, I noticed that it had a white streak along its back. Just like Silvan's streak of white hair. I believe . . .' Gilmer hesitated, swallowed and gathered his courage. 'I believe that Silvan and the Hound of

Winter may be one and the same creature!'

Jansie shouted, she wept, she all but screamed at Gilmer. She would not believe such a thing of Silvan, she cried – it was monstrous, it was mad! Hysterically, she said that she knew what Gilmer was trying to do, and she knew why, she knew *exactly* why! Gilmer saw Silvan as a rival and so was trying to poison her mind against him. But, she added furiously, if Gilmer thought for one moment that she was going to believe such cruel lies, then he was a fool, and a hateful one too!

Gilmer tried to reason with her. He wasn't trying to poison her mind, he said, but he had seen what he had seen, and to deny it would be to lie to her. What more could he do, he pleaded despairingly, than tell the truth?

At last his words got through and Jansie calmed down a little. It was unfair, she admitted, to accuse Gilmer without real evidence. But what proof did *he* have? None, Gilmer said. But there might be a way to get it. If they kept watch together tonight, and the hounds returned, they might learn more. And if he was proved wrong, Gilmer added sadly, then he would leave this house for good and never show his face to her again. That was a promise – and he didn't break his promises.

His fierce sincerity gave Jansie a twinge of conscience and, though uncomfortable, she agreed to the bargain. They would begin their vigil at midnight.

Tavia's diary was still hidden under Jansie's pillow. She had intended to tell Gilmer about it, but now was glad she hadn't. She would say nothing to anyone. Not to Gilmer; not to Silvan. She would leave the diary where it was and try not to think about it. At least, not until tonight was over . . .

'I'm not s-scared,' Jansie said through

chattering teeth. 'Just c-c-cold.'

'I understand.' It was well past midnight; they had been watching at Jansie's window for nearly two hours now and the hounds had not appeared. Gilmer didn't know whether he was sorry or relieved. For if his suspicion about Silvan was right, it would break Jansie's heart.

It was snowing yet again, but only a light and gentle fall, and the cloud was thin enough for a little moonlight to glow dimly through. Gilmer felt sleepy, and in fact his eyes were closing and he had begun to nod, when suddenly Jansie gave a sharp cry.

Instantly Gilmer was fully awake again. He looked down into the courtyard and was in time to see the front door swinging open.

Black as night, lean and menacing, the Hound of Winter emerged from the house, and with a sensation of shuddering dread, they both watched as the scene Jansie had witnessed the previous night was played over again. There was the single, soft cry, answered moments later by eldritch howls in the distance. And then, in the snow, the ghostly shapes of the white hounds racing to gather at their leader's feet. Tonight, though, there was no latecomer, for Tavia was already among them, one with the rest.

With the great black dog at their head, the hounds sped away into the night. Jansie sat motionless, tears pouring down her cheeks. Gilmer knew she was crying for her sister, and there was nothing he could say to comfort her. He stared out at the darkness, his face empty and his heart aching for her in her unhappiness.

And then the black hound returned.

It came alone, padding softly through the snow. It crossed the courtyard, climbed the steps, then stopped at the front door. Turning its head, it looked back at the silent scene, and a ripple seemed to run through the dark fur, as though a wind had stirred it. Then, as Gilmer and Jansie stared in dawning shock, the hound's form changed. Its body twisted, distorted, became longer. Its fur vanished and was replaced by clothes, while its muzzle altered into the shape of a human face – and suddenly it was no longer a hound at all, but a man, crouching on all fours at the top of the steps.

The man was Silvan.

Jansie uttered a low, agonized moan and covered her face with her hands. Gilmer saw Silvan rise to his feet, saw him slip through the front door and vanish, and something seemed to turn grey and cold inside him. There could be no doubt now. His suspicion had been proved true – Silvan *was* the Hound of Winter.

Jansie was crying again, deep, helpless sobs that stabbed Gilmer's heart. Between sobs she was trying to speak. Her voice shook and the words were barely audible, but Gilmer heard them.

'Oh, no . . . no. *It can't be. It can't. It can't!*'

Gilmer reached out, starting to say, 'Jansie –' but she drew sharply away. 'No!' With a great effort, she pulled herself together. 'I'm . . . all right.' It wasn't true, for there was a terrible, leaden pain inside her. But she had seen the truth; it couldn't be escaped or denied. And bleakly she acknowledged what she must do.

With a heavy spirit, she rose to her feet. There could be no more pretending. She – and Gilmer – had to learn all they could, whatever the personal cost.

'Gilmer,' she said softly. 'There's something else you must see. Something I found in Tavia's room.'

She took the small book from beneath her pillow. 'It's Tavia's diary,' she said. 'I don't think she can ever have shown it to anyone. But I think we must read it, Gilmer. We have no choice now.'

Chapter Eight

TAVIA HAD BEGUN her diary just a few days after her wedding. As she and Gilmer began to read it, Jansie felt a horrible pang of emotion, firstly because the words seemed to bring her sister back to life, and secondly because she felt she was intruding into something very, very private.

For the first few pages, Tavia's love for her new husband shone out like a glowing lantern. She had been so blissfully happy. But then the tone of the diary began to change.

'*I have such hideous dreams,*' Tavia had written. '*Every night they haunt me, and though Silvan says there is nothing to fear from them, I can no longer believe him. Something is wrong. Terribly wrong. And I am beginning to feel very frightened.*'

Then, on the day of the Winter Solstice, she wrote: '*The first snow fell last night. Everyone says it has come very early this year; in fact, there has been no such early fall in living memory. Silvan is very restless. We quarrelled this afternoon, and though we have made it up now, his temper is still short. But he will not tell me what troubles him.*'

Jansie shivered and turned the page. The next day's entry read: '*In the night I heard wild dogs howling. I did not know that there were such creatures here. It was a horrible sound.*'

Jansie turned again. But the next six pages were blank, and uneasily she wondered what had happened to make Tavia neglect her diary for so long. Then, on the seventh page, the writing began once more – but this time with a shocking difference, for Tavia's hand had been shaking so much that it looked as though an inky spider had scuttered across the face of the book.

'*I cannot bear it!*' she scrawled. '*It cannot be true! And yet I know it is, for I have seen him change. Silvan is not truly human – he is a monster!*'

The page blurred before Jansie's eyes. Gilmer leaned forward, one hand reaching out to take the diary away, and his voice was breaking as he said, 'Jansie –'

'No.' She interrupted him quaveringly but firmly, pulling the book out of his grasp. 'No, Gilmer. I must read it all. I *want* to.' With an effort, she made herself look at him. 'After all, I've seen the change too, haven't I? I can't deny the truth, any more than Tavia could.'

She concentrated on the diary again. There were two more blank pages and then the words began once more. Tavia was obviously calmer, for her writing had returned almost to normal. But what she wrote was stark.

'*Silvan has told me everything. He has shown me the painting in the tower, and I understand its terrible meaning. I know now why he is as he is, and why he has no choice but to do what he does . . .*' Here the page was blotted, as though Tavia had paused a long time before steeling herself to continue. Or as if she had been crying. '*. . . He has begged me to use the sword, for he says it is the only way to end his nightmare. But I cannot. Whatever manner of creature he may be, I still love him too much to do what he asks.*'

Jansie stared as her heart seemed to freeze. The sword . . . her mind flashed back to the evening when she had overheard Silvan and Tavia quarrelling in the great hall. Like a spectre in her mind, she heard Tavia's voice. '*I won't do it!*' she had cried. '*I can't!*' And when Jansie had burst into the room, Silvan had been trying to make Tavia take hold of the ancient bronze weapon . . .

Jansie turned anxiously to Gilmer, to tell him the story. But Gilmer was frowning down at the diary, and before she could speak, he said:

'The painting – of course. *Of course!*'

Jansie blinked rapidly. 'What do you mean?'

He met her gaze. 'There's a painting hanging on the wall in Silvan's tower. I've only visited the tower once, and then only for a minute, so I didn't have time to take much notice. But I've seen it. It's a very strange picture, Jansie.' He gestured towards the diary. 'Does Tavia say any more about it?'

Jansie started to turn pages, but it seemed that the rest of the book was blank . . . until suddenly, right at the end, one page had been written on.

It said: '*If Silvan could have gone away until the spring there might have been a chance. But now the snow has made travelling impossible. He has no choice but to stay. There is no hope for us. Poor Silvan. My poor, poor Silvan!*'

Jansie stared at these last sentences. 'I don't understand . . .' she said softly. '"If Silvan could have gone away" – what can that mean?'

Gilmer shook his head. 'I don't know. But do you remember how anxious he was when we arrived? How impatient to leave on his journey?' He hunched his shoulders ominously. 'He said he had to go away on business, but I think his real reason must have been very different. And then the big snowfall came, and he was trapped here.'

My poor, poor Silvan, Tavia had written. And Jansie felt those sad words like a blade in her own heart. She couldn't hate Silvan for what he was. Like Tavia, she felt desperate pity for him . . . and desperate love.

She turned to Gilmer and said, 'There must be a way to help him! If we could –'

Gilmer interrupted before she could say any more. '*Help* him?' he echoed incredulously. 'Jansie, how can we or anyone else possibly help him? He isn't a man, he's a monster! Tavia said it herself, and you can't deny what you've seen with your own eyes! Silvan is dangerous!'

'No!' Jansie protested. 'He can't help himself, I know he can't! He isn't evil!'

'Jansie,' Gilmer said, 'Silvan killed his own wife. He killed your sister!'

They quarrelled then, and only the sudden realization that their raised voices might wake the servants brought the quarrel to an end. As they sat in tense, angry silence, Gilmer remembered that this was the second argument they had had in less than a day. The last thing he wanted in the world was to clash with Jansie, but it seemed there was no choice. For his conscience wouldn't allow him to agree with her, or even to pretend to. As far as he was concerned, Silvan was a dangerous creature. But love had blinded Jansie. And her blindness could lead her into terrible danger.

Jansie stood up suddenly and said in a

stiff voice, 'Gilmer, I want you to go now. I wish you a good night.'

Gilmer sighed, but he didn't argue. There was no point. He had nothing left to say, and he went to his room.

Jansie didn't sleep that night. She had expected to cry again, but tears didn't come; instead she lay awake, staring into the dark, thinking.

Whatever Gilmer thought, whatever he believed about Silvan, Jansie was utterly convinced he was wrong, and her heart ached with grief for her brother-in-law. Silvan *wasn't* evil. Tavia had known the truth about him, and she had still loved him. And even if Silvan *had* killed his wife – which was something Jansie wouldn't yet let herself believe – then he must have been unaware of what he was doing. He must, she thought, be under a curse. It was the only possible explanation. And she was determined to find a way to help him.

She thought about the painting that

hung in Silvan's tower. In her diary Tavia had written of understanding 'its terrible meaning'. If Jansie, too, could understand, would it tell her the whole story or simply pose yet another conundrum? Somehow, Jansie thought, she must visit the tower in secret and look for herself. It wouldn't be easy, for Silvan spent much of his time there. But if she waited, a chance would come.

It came, in fact, far sooner than she could have hoped, for shortly after dawn, she heard footsteps on the landing and peeped from her room to see Silvan going towards the stairs. Barefoot, and ignoring the cold that struck up through the soles of her feet, Jansie tiptoed along the corridor and looked over the banisters. Silvan was in the hall below, talking to a servant, and she heard him say, 'Well, then, if the snow's cleared a little, you'd best go to the village for fresh supplies. I'll walk round the grounds for a while; send someone to find me when you return.'

Jansie's pulse quickened. Silvan was going out, and from the sound of it, would not be back for some time. This was the perfect opportunity!

She dressed hastily, and ran towards the staircase that led to the tower room. The staircase was dark and she hadn't brought a candle; as the door swung to behind her, the shadows closed in like predators . . . like hounds, she thought with a shudder, and tried to thrust the thought away. Her face and hands were perspiring and her nerve almost failed, but with an effort she started to climb. Round and round the stairs curved in a spiral, and the darkness grew more intense until she was groping blindly in black gloom.

At last she reached the top of the stairs. Before her was a heavy door, but to her relief it wasn't locked and so she stepped into Silvan's private sanctum.

There were two narrow windows, which let in enough light to see clearly. The room was sparsely furnished with only a table, chair and lamp. And on the wall was the painting.

Very strange and stylized, the picture showed the figure of a tall, black-haired man, standing in a snow-filled forest clearing and looking down at the body of a huge black dog that lay at his feet. The animal was snarling, but there was blood on its fur and it was clearly badly wounded. The man was brandishing a bronze sword, holding it poised above the dog's throat as though about to strike a death-blow.

Jansie stared at the painting in horrified fascination. She recognized the sword instantly – it was the one that hung over the mantel in the great hall. The dog, too, was horribly familiar, and she shuddered as she remembered the beast that had attacked her in her room, and Silvan's terrible transformation last night. But the man himself . . . she couldn't be sure who he was, for in the painting he was looking down and his face was obscured. But the black hair, the height . . . it must be

Silvan, she thought. Silvan, killing the Hound of Winter . . .

Then her breath caught in her throat as she saw that there were other figures in the picture. At first she hadn't seen them, for they were like ghosts among the trees, faint and pale and spectral. Young girls, twelve or more of them. Some were dark, others fair, and their faces were deathly white as though all the blood had been drained from them. And each one was dressed in a long, white shift, like a shroud . . .

Then Jansie saw the last figure. It was unfinished, as though the artist had run out of paint or simply given up before he had completed his work. Her face and figure were nothing more than a sketched outline and only a little of her white shift had been painted in.

But the paint, she saw suddenly, was wet.

Jansie's heart began to pound agonizingly. The painting bore a signature, in tiny lettering, in one corner of the canvas. She hadn't looked at it before, but now she forced herself to move closer and study it. But she believed she already knew what she would see, and she was right. The artist was Silvan himself.

Slowly, Jansie stepped back from the picture. She felt sick, and a terrible suspicion was growing in her mind. This picture was very old, she could tell, for in places the paint was cracked and dulled like the ancient ancestral portraits in her parents' house. So if Silvan had painted it all, when had he begun it?

She started to back away from the painting and realized suddenly that she wanted above all else to get out of this grim room. The atmosphere seemed to be closing in on her, and fear was crawling in her veins and bringing a choking sensation to her throat. She didn't understand the story that the painting told, but suddenly she was terrified of it, and of what it might mean. For if her suspicion was right, then Silvan must be at least two hundred years old.

Jansie turned and fled from the tower. She didn't even think about the horrors of the dark staircase; all that mattered was to get out, get away. By the time she reached the landing, she was shuddering uncontrollably, and she ran towards the stairs without so much as a backward glance.

And so she didn't see the shadow that stood silently at the far end of the corridor. She didn't see the green eyes that had watched her emerge from the door at the foot of the spiral stairs. And she didn't see or hear Silvan move soft-footed from his hiding-place and take another route to the ground floor and the gardens beyond.

Chapter Nine

THE SERVANT SILVAN had sent to the village came back later that morning with grim news to tell. Last night, he said, there had been another attack on a flock of sheep that was grazing at the edge of the forest. Five animals had been found with their throats torn out. And dogs had been heard howling in the deep of the night.

Jansie had recovered from the worst of her fright, and she and Gilmer were both in the kitchen. She had told him nothing of what had happened to her, but as she heard the servant's story, she felt something inside her constrict again with unease. Gilmer looked pointedly at her, but she refused to meet his gaze; she only turned away and pretended to be busy. But later, as they were leaving the great hall after a silent and stilted lunch (at which Silvan was present but barely said a word), he seized the chance to speak to her alone.

'Jansie!' Gilmer's urgent hiss stopped Jansie in her tracks. She turned, saw him, and her face became hostile. 'What do you want, Gilmer?'

'I have to talk to you!'

She shook her head. 'There's nothing to say.'

'I think there is.' Gilmer was angry, she realized – or afraid. 'Jansie, after the news that came from the village this morning, we *can't* let this go on! Five more sheep dead, and you and I both know that this is only the beginning.

How many more animals will the hounds kill if they're not stopped? And how long will it be before they grow tired of animals and start killing *people*?' He paused. 'Just the way Silvan killed Tavia.'

'We don't know that he did!' Jansie's voice broke sharply from her throat. 'We don't know anything for certain, and I won't listen to any more of this, Gilmer! I don't want to hear it, do you understand?'

And with that she strode away.

Gilmer stared after her, wondering at her stubbornness. Surely she couldn't deny the truth, now that she had seen it so starkly for herself? Love, he thought sorrowfully, could be a terrifyingly powerful emotion at times. As he knew to his own cost . . .

He turned at last and walked away in the opposite direction. And Silvan, who unbeknown to either Gilmer or Jansie had been standing just inside the half-open door of the great hall, watched his departing back with narrowed, unquiet eyes.

Jansie contrived to avoid Gilmer for the rest of the day, and finally the young herbalist gave up his efforts to reason with her. He hoped that once she had had time to think more deeply, she might come round to his point of view. But until and unless that happened, there was nothing he could do to persuade her.

Jansie, however, had no intention of being persuaded, by Gilmer or anyone else. Only one thing mattered to her – her beloved Silvan. She *had* to learn more. She *had* to find out the truth behind Silvan's terrible secret, and search for a way to help him. And when, as usual, Silvan disappeared to the tower room later that morning, she began her search in earnest.

There had been no more snowfalls since the previous night, but the sky was an ominous leaden colour and great cloud-banks were starting to build up in the north. A fire had been lit in the great hall that morning but had almost died to nothing by afternoon, and Jansie shivered as she tiptoed into the deserted, echoing room and approached the mantel. There, hanging in its usual place and glimmering dully – threateningly, she thought – was the bronze sword. Jansie stared at it for several minutes and then, gathering her courage, pulled a chair to the hearth, climbed on to it and lifted down the sword.

It was tremendously heavy and she almost dropped it. Resting it on the chair, she looked at the ancient weapon more closely. The ominous words etched into the metal seemed to glower at her, and she touched them with light, uneasy fingers.

'*I was your salvation. And I shall be your doom . . .*' Her own voice echoed uncannily in the emptiness as softly she repeated the chilling sentences aloud. She thought of the painting in the tower room, the snarling hound, the stabbing blade. Salvation and doom. Silvan killing the Hound of Winter – killing *himself*. She had to look at the painting again, Jansie told herself. She had to try, somehow, to understand the story that it told. If Silvan came down to dinner tonight that might give her an opportunity. She could only pray that he wouldn't decide to stay in the tower.

Jansie's prayers were answered, and Silvan did join her and Gilmer at dinner. The soup was eaten in silence, and as the servant cleared away and prepared to bring the second course Jansie made her move.

'I'm sorry,' she said, 'but I have a dreadful headache and I really couldn't eat any more.' She gave Silvan an apologetic smile that made Gilmer's heart turn over. 'I think I'd better go and lie down in my room.'

Silvan said of course, she must do just

as she wished. Gilmer asked if she would like a herbal cure but Jansie said no, and the two men watched her leave the room. The main course was served – it was fish, and delicious, but to Gilmer it might as well have been scraps from the kitchen bins – and then suddenly Silvan pushed his plate away and stood up.

'To be honest, Gilmer, I'm not feeling too well myself.' He frowned. 'Perhaps it was the mutton we ate at lunchtime; I suspect it might have disagreed with me. That's probably what's wrong with Jansie, too.'

'I feel well enough,' Gilmer said.

'Maybe your stomach is hardier.' Silvan smiled, though the smile wasn't reflected in his eyes, which looked very cold. 'I'll follow Jansie's example, I think, and lie down for a while. Perhaps you'll tell the cook to throw the mutton away if there's any left. Better to be on the safe side.'

'Yes,' said Gilmer. 'Yes, I will.'

Silvan left, and Gilmer stared at the closed door for several minutes. His own food was going cold but now he didn't feel like eating. Something was *wrong*. Impossible to put a finger on it, but Gilmer had an uneasy feeling in his bones, like an itch that wouldn't go away. Silvan's words hadn't quite rung true; in fact Gilmer didn't believe for one moment that there was anything wrong with him. Did he have some reason for wanting to follow Jansie . . .?

Suddenly he was out of his chair and running across the room. Opening the door he peered out and saw a maid crossing the hall.

'Where are Miss Jansie and Master Silvan?' he asked.

The maid turned. 'Miss Jansie's in her room, Master Gilmer. And Master Silvan went up to the tower just now.'

Gilmer felt foolish as he realized he had been seeing demons where none existed. Silvan hadn't followed Jansie.

Maybe he wasn't really ill but was just making an excuse to hide the fact that he didn't want any food. And if he and his creatures had slaughtered five sheep last night, Gilmer thought cynically, that was hardly surprising.

He went back into the great hall and began half-heartedly to pick at his own meal. At least, he told himself, Jansie was safe for the time being.

He didn't know how wrong he was.

Convinced that Silvan would stay in the hall with Gilmer for a good hour yet, Jansie had gone back to her room to fetch Tavia's diary and then made her way to the spiral stairs. Knowing now what awaited her in the tower, she was a little less frightened by the stairs' foreboding atmosphere, but none the less her pulse was racing and her stomach churning by the time she reached the door of Silvan's sanctum and pushed it open.

In the light of her candle the painting

had an unearthly look to it. The wounded hound seemed so real that she could almost believe it might at any minute spring to snarling life. And the man wielding the sword looked dark and strange, like something from a nightmare. Shivering, and telling herself it was only the chill, Jansie crossed the floor – then froze.

Something about the painting was different. For a few moments she couldn't be sure what it was, then suddenly she realized. The last figure, which this morning had been only a vague outline, was almost complete. The new paint gleamed wetly. The white shroud. The pallid face. The golden hair. The blue eyes . . .

It was Tavia.

Jansie gave a cry of dismay. 'Oh, no! He can't –'

But she got no further, for from behind her came a shocking sound: the noise of the door being slammed shut. Jansie's cry became a squeak of terror;

she spun round –

And Silvan, his green eyes like ice-cold jewels in the gloom, said, 'Ah, Jansie. So you know. I had hoped it wouldn't have to come to this . . .'

Chapter Ten

IN A SINGLE moment of panic Jansie
looked into Silvan's eyes and knew
that she had only one chance. She
didn't pause, didn't think; she just
hurled herself forward and raced for the
door.

She reached it – but as her fingers
clawed for the latch a hand with
tremendous strength snatched hold of
her arm and spun her off her feet. Jansie
screamed – little use, for who could hear
her up here? – and crashed against the
wall. She slid to the floor, and as she

tried to struggle upright she saw Silvan advance menacingly towards her.

'Silvan, no . . . please . . .' Jansie shrank back, her eyes wide with horror. Silvan had turned from the man she loved into a deadly stranger. A stranger who wasn't even human . . .

He reached for her, and something in Jansie snapped. With a shout of fear she jack-knifed upright and made a second bid for freedom. Silvan was too quick for her. He grabbed hold of her wrists as she tried to rush past him, and they staggered, struggling, back and forth across the room. Jansie fought like a wildcat but Silvan was far stronger than she was. She was sure he was going to kill her, and there was nothing she could do to stop him –

But then suddenly Silvan broke away. Jansie reeled, clutched at the edge of the table, and stared at him in astonishment. His rage had gone, and in its place was torment.

Softly, sorrowfully, Silvan said, 'You

shouldn't have meddled, Jansie. You shouldn't have pried.'

And then, to her amazement, he covered his face with his hands and started to sob.

Instantly all Jansie's terror was swept away by a surge of love and pity so powerful that it snatched the breath from her throat. She ran to him, arms outstretched, and her voice broke as she cried, 'Oh, Silvan!'

Silvan caught hold of her. His arms went round her and he crushed her against him. Jansie felt the hardness of his ribs, felt the pounding of his heart, and her mind swam with a dizzying blend of shock and delight. This was what she had dreamed of for so long, to be in Silvan's arms, embraced by him, wanted, *needed* –

He whispered her name, his voice so tortured that tears sprang to Jansie's eyes too. Then – she hadn't expected it, though she had prayed it might happen – his face was close to hers and he was kissing her. The kiss seemed to go on for ever, but when finally it ended Jansie was almost sobbing with grief and joy mingled confusingly together. But there was no joy in Silvan's eyes when he looked at her, and slowly her happiness melted away as she gazed at his face.

'You know, don't you?' he said. 'You know the truth about me.'

Jansie turned away. She couldn't bear to say the word. But Silvan said it for her.

'Yes. You know.' He paused. 'Have you . . . seen? Seen what happens to me?'

She nodded, still unable to speak. Silvan sighed bitterly.

'Whatever you might think of me, Jansie, I'm not truly evil. But I can't expect you to believe that, can I?'

Startled, Jansie did look at him this time. 'Silvan, you don't understand!' She shook her head wildly. 'I don't hate you, and I don't hold you to blame! I want to *help* you! If there's a way, any way at all, then I want to take it, because –' Then Jansie stopped abruptly. She had been about to say, 'because I love you', but even as the words came to her tongue she knew that she could not, *must* not, utter them.

Silvan stared at her. His face was still strained, his eyes still had a strange, hard edge. But there was a new light in them. The light of hope.

'Jansie,' he said, 'there is a way to help me. Tavia couldn't do it, though I begged her to. But if you're strong enough –'

'I'm strong!' Jansie said fiercely.

'Yes. Yes, I know you are. But even you might not be strong enough for this.' He hesitated. 'I'll tell you my story, Jansie. All of it. And then, perhaps, you'll truly understand . . .'

Many years ago, Silvan said, he was a mortal man like any other, and had lived happily in this house with his beautiful young wife. In those days he often went hunting, for there were wild wolves in the district that preyed on the sheep-flocks and, as overlord, it was Silvan's duty to protect his tenants' farms.

But then strange rumours began. A new kind of wild beast had begun to terrorize the district: not a wolf but something else, a hideous black hound with burning eyes. People went in dread of the creature, saying that it was no normal animal but a supernatural monster, and they begged Silvan to hunt it down and kill it.

'For more than a month I searched for it in the forest,' Silvan told Jansie, 'but I could never find it. It was cunning – unnaturally cunning. It knew that I had set out to destroy it. And one night, it . . .' His voice caught in his throat; he faltered and then forced himself to go on. '. . . one night, it turned the tables on me.'

'How?' Jansie asked softly.

'It was the night before the Winter Solstice, and the snow was falling early,'

Silvan continued. 'I knew that snow would make it easier to track the hound, so I went to the forest again, determined to find and kill it at last. I found its trail and followed it. But the trail led back to my house. And there, in the courtyard, I found the body of my wife.'

There was a moment's silence, and the shadows of the tower room seemed to close around Jansie like a shroud. Then, so quietly that she could barely hear him, Silvan said:

'The hound had entered my house. It found my wife alone, and it dragged her outside and tore out her throat.'

Like a grim, tragic tapestry unfolding, Silvan told the story of the revenge he had taken on the Hound of Winter. In a frenzy of grief and rage he had taken the bronze sword, which had been his grandfather's, and returned to the forest. He followed the hound for a night and a day, and finally cornered it in its lair. But as the blade of the sword pierced its heart, the monster did not howl as any normal animal would have done. Instead, it laughed with a human voice. And it spoke. In the moments before it died, it used its supernatural powers to put a curse upon Silvan – that he would take its place and become the new Hound of Winter.

'I can hear those words now,' Silvan said brokenly, covering his face with his hands and shuddering. 'It said, "You cannot defeat me, human hunter, for I will live on in you. And each year, if snow should fall on the Winter Solstice, you will become what I have been, and you will hunger for the blood of those you love, and you will kill them. And when you have killed them, they too will be as you are."'

Jansie's eyes widened as the hideous truth dawned on her. 'The blood of those you love . . .' she whispered. 'Then the white hounds are . . .'

Silvan nodded slowly. 'This curse has been on me for two hundred years. The white hounds are all the girls I have loved, and married, and murdered, through the centuries of my life.'

So many times, Silvan said, he had been foolish enough to believe that the hound's dying bane would not fall upon him again. When winter followed winter and no snow fell on the Solstice, he had dared to think that he was safe. Many times he had fallen in love; many times he had married. But then another winter would bring early snow. And Silvan was doomed to be half man and half monster – and to kill the girl he loved.

He had meant to go away this time, he said. There was a chance, just a chance, that if he travelled far from his home then Tavia would be safe until spring came again and the curse released its grim hold on him. But the blizzard on the night of Jansie's arrival had trapped him here. So he had asked Tavia to do the one thing that could save them both – and she had refused.

As these words were spoken, Jansie's pulse raced in her veins and her hands shook. She believed she knew what Silvan had asked of Tavia. And when he spoke again, her belief was confirmed.

'There is only one way to break the curse,' Silvan said quietly. 'And that is to take the bronze sword – the same sword with which I killed the Hound of Winter – and pierce me through the heart.' He looked at Jansie then, and a dreadful, intense fire burned in the depths of his green eyes. 'I pleaded with Tavia to do it; to release me and give me the peace I crave. She couldn't. She said that she loved me too much. But oh, Jansie, if Tavia had understood my torment she would have done what I asked. For my sake, she would have found the strength.'

An awful sense of dismay began to rise in Jansie, for she knew then what Silvan was about to say to her. When he reached out to take hold of her hands she wanted to pull away. But her feelings were too powerful. She wanted him to touch her. She wanted him to love her . . .

'Jansie,' Silvan began. 'I beg you, please –'

'*No!*' Suddenly Jansie's voice cracked from her throat and she whirled away from him, snatching her hands free and thrusting them shudderingly through her hair. She felt as if her mind was splitting apart. 'Silvan, no – don't ask it of me!' Tears started to stream down her face. 'I can't do it! I can't kill you!'

'Jansie, I *want* to die! You're my only hope now.'

'But I'm not!' Jansie sobbed. 'Tavia couldn't do it because she loved you too much. But I – oh, Silvan, don't you understand? I can't do it either, because I love you just as she did!'

There was a long silence. Then: 'Yes,' said Silvan. 'I know.'

Very slowly Jansie turned to face him. 'You know?'

His expression was anguished. 'You tried to hide it, but your eyes told me the truth. And that's why I ask this of you, Jansie – for, you see, my life can only be ended by someone who *does* truly love me.' He hesitated. 'Someone like Tavia – or you.'

Jansie said nothing. She felt as if her heart was being torn apart, for the despair in Silvan's voice told her that, above all else in the world, he wanted to die. Yet she wanted him to live, with a yearning that was a physical pain within her. There had to be another way. There *had* to be!

'I tried desperately to stop myself from harming Tavia,' Silvan continued quietly. 'But when the change comes upon me ... I'm insane. I'm not human. I'm a monster, just like the monster I stabbed all those years ago. I killed her. And now I'm so afraid that I'll kill you, too. Please, Jansie, *please* – take the sword and use it!'

Yet though Silvan pleaded with all his strength, Jansie knew she couldn't do what he wanted. Surely, she argued, there must be another means of breaking the curse? Silvan said no. Only his death would end it. But still she couldn't agree. Finally Silvan pleaded with her at least to lock him in the tower room every night, so that when the change came over him she would be safe.

'It only happens during the hours of darkness,' he told her, 'and only on nights when snow is falling. It isn't ideal, Jansie. I might break out. But at least this way there's a chance for you.'

Jansie agreed, though reluctantly. Then Silvan glanced towards the window.

'It's getting late.' He suppressed a shiver. 'There are clouds building up, and it might snow tonight. You'd better go, quickly.' From his coat pocket he brought a heavy key. 'Lock the door behind you. And whatever you do, whatever you might hear, don't open it again until morning.'

Cold, invisible hands seemed to clutch at Jansie's spine, and as she took the key her hand was shaking. She turned to Silvan one last time, bewilderment and pain in her eyes, and suddenly he caught hold of her again, drawing her to him. His second kiss was gentle, very emotional, and when at last they broke apart he said sadly:

'Oh, Jansie . . . if only my life had been different. For I believe I could have loved you very dearly.'

She looked back as she left the room. But Silvan had turned away and was gazing out of the window. And the shadows of the future seemed to be gathering in the tower room.

Chapter Eleven

GILMER FOUND JANSIE crying her heart out in the great hall. She hadn't meant anyone to see her; the servants were all in the kitchen and she had thought herself safe from discovery. Gilmer took one look at her pale, tear-stained face, strode across the room and dropped to a crouch beside her chair.

'Jansie!' Alarm filled his voice. 'Jansie, whatever's wrong?'

Jansie shook her head, unable to speak, and turned her face away. But

Gilmer wasn't going to be put off. Their earlier quarrel forgotten, he reached out and took hold of her hands. Then suddenly Jansie's resistance gave way and she found herself sobbing in his arms.

'Oh, Gilmer . . .' Her voice was muffled as she pressed her head against his shoulder. 'What am I going to do? What am I going to do?'

Jansie had been determined not to confide the hideous truth of what she had learned to anyone, and after the earlier bitterness between them Gilmer was the last person in the world she wanted to tell. But inside, she was hurting so much. Hurting with grief, with pity, and with fear both for Silvan and for herself. She couldn't bear to carry the burden of her feelings alone. Gilmer was so kind, so concerned and – though the thought made her feel horribly guilty – so loving to her, that almost before she knew it her resolve crumbled and she told him everything.

Gilmer was horrified. 'Jansie, I know how you feel about Silvan,' he said, with a sharp edge to his voice. 'But those feelings have made you blind to sense. Silvan has to die!'

'*No* –' Jansie started to protest, but Gilmer interrupted.

'Yes! I'm not going to stand by and wait for you to become another one of his victims!'

'He won't hurt me!'

'He told you himself, when he changes into the Hound he has no control over what he does. He could kill you in a moment!' Gilmer drew a harsh breath. 'It's no use, Jansie, you won't persuade me. If you can't bring yourself to use that sword as he asks, then I can and must – for your sake!'

Tears were streaming down Jansie's face again. She hated herself for showing such weakness in front of Gilmer, and suddenly she felt bitterly angry.

'You can't hurt Silvan!' she fired

back. 'Only someone who truly loves him can kill him with the sword. And –' her lip curled and she almost sneered at him '– that certainly isn't you, Gilmer!'

Gilmer stared back at her with a mixture of pain and fury in his expression. Then abruptly he got to his feet.

'I've had enough of this,' he said ferociously. 'I'm trying to *help* you, Jansie! I'm trying to stop you from going where Tavia has already gone! But if you're determined to be stupid as well as blind, then there's no point my saying anything at all.' He started towards the door, then stopped and looked back at her again. 'But you might do well to remember two things. Firstly, Silvan *wants* to die. Killing him would be a mercy for him as well as for you. And secondly, even if the sword won't work for me, maybe there's another way.'

And he left the room.

For a long time after he had gone, Jansie sat motionless on her chair. The candles in the hall were burning low and shadows were creeping in on her, but she didn't notice – or didn't care.

What had Gilmer meant by his last words? What would he do? What *could* he do? She didn't know the answer. But she was suddenly very frightened.

A noise behind her made her start, and she turned to see that a servant had come in.

'Oh, beg pardon, Miss Jansie. I thought it would be a good idea to build up the fire.'

'Oh. Yes,' said Jansie in a faraway voice.

The servant paused, frowning. 'Is everything all right, miss?'

'Yes. Yes, thank you.'

Wood clattered, followed by the noise of the fire being raked. 'We all thought it was going to snow again,' the servant said, 'but now the sky is clearing and the stars are out. It's going to be a very cold night, so I'll make sure there's a good blaze in your room and –'

Jansie interrupted then. 'What did you say?'

'That I'll make sure there's –'

'No. About the stars.' She had started to tremble. 'Did you say the sky's clearing? That there won't be any snow tonight?'

'That's right, miss. And a blessing it'll be, too.'

'Yes.' Jansie thought of Silvan in the locked tower room, and a surge of dizzy relief washed over her. Tonight, at least, there would be no transformation. 'Yes,' she said again. 'It *will* be a blessing.'

Although the change in the weather kept one of Jansie's terrors at bay, the other and greater terror haunted her as she lay in bed that night. Try as she might, she couldn't sleep. All she could think of was Gilmer and his threat.

The night sky was still clear. Up in the tower, she knew, Silvan would also be awake, pacing the small room like a caged animal. The key to the tower was under her pillow, so Gilmer could do nothing to harm Silvan tonight. But tomorrow might be another matter . . .

Jansie stared into the dark. How could Gilmer try to kill Silvan? And then a terrible possibility occurred to her: there were many herbs in the house, and Gilmer knew how to use them. She imagined Silvan poisoned and dying in agony . . .

The house was creaking as it so often did at night, the rafters that were its bones shifting and flexing. Outside, the wind was moaning, sounding like a soul in torment. Jansie shivered and snuggled deeper into her blankets. She didn't want to believe the worst of Gilmer, but the risk of trusting him was too great. Something had to be done. And she could think of only one way.

Jansie got up as soon as the first signs of

an icy, dismal dawn showed in the east. In the kitchen the servants were surprised to see her so early, and even more surprised when she ordered them to gather up every herb in the house and bring them to her. But they didn't argue, and when the herbs were brought, Jansie burned them all on the kitchen fire. Gilmer would be furious, but Jansie no longer cared what he or anyone thought. All that mattered to her was Silvan. And when the fire had consumed the last of the herbs, she climbed up to the tower and unlocked the door of Silvan's room.

All he said to Jansie was, 'Thank you . . .'

She knew what he meant, knew there was no need for any further words, and she went quietly downstairs again. Her heart was aching, for she wished so much that there had been something more – a touch, even a kiss. But the unhappiness in Silvan's tired eyes told her that it couldn't be. Not yet. Not until and unless his despair could be turned to hope.

Gilmer came down to the kitchen a short while later. Jansie knew she couldn't hide what she had done, and was ready for the quarrel that she felt must follow. But Gilmer didn't react with the fury she expected. Instead, he stood for a moment in the middle of the floor, one hand pressed to his forehead as though he was fighting some great emotion. Then he turned and, without a word, left the kitchen.

Jansie stared after him. Had she misjudged him? Guilt filled her. But what other choice had there been? She couldn't have taken the risk, Jansie told herself. She *couldn't*.

Jansie spent the day in a fog of misery. Gilmer avoided her, and Silvan stayed alone in his tower room. She longed for him to come down, to talk with her, simply *be* with her, but only as the sun was setting did he at last emerge.

Gilmer didn't join them for dinner. Silvan was curious at his absence but Jansie made no attempt to explain. Then, as dusk fell, a new bank of cloud began to pile up ominously in the sky. Tonight, it would snow again.

Silvan, too, had seen the worsening weather, and as the meal progressed he grew more and more tense. At last he got up, went to the window and stared out before speaking in a sharp, uneasy voice.

'The snow will start falling very soon. I must go to the tower, Jansie.' His green eyes filled with pain. 'Tonight whatever happens, whatever you hear or whatever you feel, you *must* not open that door.'

Jansie nodded wretchedly. 'I understand, Silvan.'

Up the spiral stairs again and to the cheerless room. Jansie watched Silvan go in and wanted so much to say something that would comfort him. But the words wouldn't come, and she turned the key in the lock and went sadly downstairs once more.

For two hours she sat by the fire in the great hall. It wasn't snowing yet but the clouds were now a solid pall blotting out the moon and stars. The snow would begin falling at any moment, and she tried desperately not to think of Silvan imprisoned in the tower. Then there was a knock at the door and one of the maids came in.

'Miss Jansie, do you know where Master Gilmer is?' the maid asked. 'I can't find him anywhere.'

'*No*,' Jansie said. 'I haven't seen him since . . .' Then abruptly her voice tailed off. Gilmer, not in the house? Where was he, then? And an awful intuition took hold of her. She had destroyed Gilmer's herbs – but there was a herbalist in the village on the other side of the forest, who would have fresh supplies. Was that where Gilmer had gone . . .?

'Oh, no . . .' She stood up quickly,

heart pounding, then swung to face the maid.

'We've got to find him!' she said, feeling the terror rise in her. 'And quickly – *quickly*!'

Chapter Twelve

A SWIFT SEARCH of the stables confirmed Jansie's fear. Gilmer's horse had gone. And when she looked outside, she saw a fresh line of hoofprints leading away to the forest.

Jansie stood in the middle of the courtyard as a feeling of blind fury washed over her. *How could Gilmer be so treacherous?* she thought bitterly. She had to see Silvan! Each morning he had breakfast sent to him in the tower room; that would be the perfect chance for Gilmer to strike. Whatever happened, he must not succeed – Silvan had to be warned!

A white flake spiralled down from the sky and landed softly, coldly on her face. Then another, and another. The snow was beginning to fall again, and with an inward stab of horror Jansie turned and ran, back into the gloomy house, through the hall and up the stairs towards Silvan's tower.

'Silvan!' She hammered on the door, crying his name. But there was no response.

'Silvan, answer me! *Please!*' Was he sleeping? Surely her shouts would wake him! But still there came no sound from beyond the door.

Frantically, and entirely forgetting Silvan's earlier warning, Jansie scrabbled for the key, thrust it into the lock and turned it. The lock clicked; she swung the door open, calling Silvan's name again –

And the call choked off into a gasp of horror as she came face to face with a living nightmare.

Silvan was crouching on the floor, his back pressed against the wall. But the form that confronted Jansie was no longer that of a human being. His face was a monstrous, twisted mask – nose becoming an animal's muzzle, mouth stretching wide and filled with yellow fangs, eyes blazing with an insane glare. His clothes were transforming into rippling black fur, and his body writhed wildly as though in the grip of some terrible fit. Jansie was too late; with the start of the snowfall, the curse had woken to hideous life, and Silvan was turning into the Hound of Winter!

As the full impact of the confrontation hit her, Jansie froze motionless in the doorway. But her paralysis lasted only a moment. For with a violent movement Silvan's head came up. He saw her – and from his throat came a hideous snarl.

Jansie screamed, 'No, *no! Silvan!*' But Silvan was beyond understanding. Half man and half animal, his mind was in the grip of complete madness, and as Jansie tried to flee through the door he sprang at her. She had a horrifying glimpse of his hands – now covered in long black fur, and with raking claws where his nails had once been – and then his fingers clamped around her throat in a deadly, strangling grip.

Jansie struggled frantically and they swayed across the room together, crashing against the table. Blood rushed to Jansie's head and a red mist started to blur her vision – but through its veils, she saw Silvan's eyes. Behind the rabid crimson glare of the Hound, the human part of him was battling against the curse with all its strength. And he was terrified.

Jansie knew she had only one slender chance. With renewed strength she fought against his stranglehold and, briefly, his grip loosened enough for her to find her voice.

'*Silvan!*' she gasped. '*Silvan, no, don't – I'm not your enemy!*'

Silvan's hands had been tightening on her throat again, but as she cried out, he paused. His grotesque face took on an expression of pure agony as he seemed to realize what he was doing. But the power of the curse was too strong, and his fingers started to squeeze –

'Silvan!' Jansie screamed. 'Gilmer's gone to the village – he means to get poison, to kill you–'

She didn't know why she was telling him; she was simply babbling words, anything she could think of that might break through his madness and reach him. But she got no further than that, for with an awful sound that was half shriek and half snarl Silvan flung her aside. Jansie cannoned into the wall, rebounded and fell sprawling to the floor. As she dizzily raised her head she saw the final change come over Silvan. All traces of humanity vanished, but for one last thing – a wild, evil laugh. Then, like a dark streak, he leaped over her and raced from the room.

Jansie scrabbled to her feet and staggered to the door. Desperately she cried Silvan's name, but he was gone. Breath rasping in her throat, which still ached from his strangling clutch, Jansie stumbled down the spiral staircase, on to the landing, down the main staircase. Half-way down she saw that the front door stood wide open. Silvan – or the Hound – had fled out into the night.

Jansie gulped more air into her lungs and ran down the last of the stairs and into the kitchen. There was no time to explain anything. 'I want my horse saddled!' she ordered. '*Hurry!*'

As a servant obeyed, Jansie raced to the great hall. Her mind was in turmoil and she hardly knew what she was doing; all she could think of was that suddenly the tables had been turned. Gilmer had set out to kill Silvan, but now Silvan meant to kill Gilmer. She had to do something!

The ancient bronze sword hung in its place above the mantel. Jansie heaved down the weapon and headed for the front door, clutching it. Minutes later the groom appeared, leading her horse. He was anxious, asking questions, but Jansie brushed them aside as he helped her into the saddle. She had no cloak and only slippers on her feet, but she didn't care. She had to catch up with Silvan!

Other servants emerged from the house, calling out to her, perplexed to see her carrying the sword. Jansie was about to shout back that she would explain later when she heard a sound that chilled her to the marrow. Far away, but carrying clearly on the ice-cold air, it was the long-drawn howling of a pack of dogs . . .

Jansie gave a yell that sent the groom jumping backwards in shock, and dug her heels into the horse's flanks. It sprang away with a whinny, and with the snow flying in her face Jansie went galloping out of the courtyard.

*

Careless of her own safety in the darkness and the whirling snow, Jansie rode at breakneck speed towards the forest. If Silvan had left footprints they were already covered, but she knew where the track to the village was and felt certain that he must have gone that way.

Tears streamed down her face as she rode, freezing into icy crystals on her cheeks. The tears were for Silvan, for Gilmer, for Tavia – and for herself. The shock of seeing Silvan's transformation, and of his savage attack on her, had thrown her emotions into new turmoil. Oh, she still loved him. Just as Tavia and all the other doomed girls had loved him. But warring with that love was another feeling – a feeling for Gilmer. She didn't want him to die, any more than she wanted Silvan to die. But if Silvan should catch up with him, then Gilmer's life would end. She had to stop it. *She had to!*

The forest loomed ahead in the night,

looking like a dark, ominous sea rolling towards her. The snow became deeper, and then they were in among the trees and a greater darkness engulfed them. The horse was nervous, jinking at shadows, and Jansie looked fearfully to left and right, hoping yet dreading to catch a glimpse of a dark, sleek shape moving among the pines.

Then, far off, she heard the howling again.

Jansie jerked on the reins, bringing her horse to a stop. The animal's ears were pricked forward and she could feel it trembling as she strained to listen. For a moment there was only the rustling patter of the snow falling. Then, so suddenly that she almost jolted out of the saddle, a wild and savage snarl echoed from somewhere just ahead of her. A single shriek rang out – not human, but the scream of a terrified horse – and on its heels came a sudden commotion, somebody shouting . . .

A shape exploded from the darkness

ahead, careering towards Jansie. She had only a moment in which to see and recognize Gilmer's riderless horse before it had bolted past her and away into the night, and a cry of horror broke from her lips.

'*Silvan!*'

Her own horse was rearing in panic; ferociously she hauled its head around, bringing it under control, then drove her heels hard into its sides. Silvan and Gilmer – she had to reach them in time, had to stop Silvan from tearing Gilmer's throat out –

She didn't see the low-hanging branch. All she knew was that something struck her arm a violent blow and the next instant she was pitching backwards out of the saddle. The world spun – trees seemed to tumble towards her, then a huge, white wall came rushing to meet her, and with a terrific impact her consciousness was blotted out.

Chapter Thirteen

JANSIE OPENED HER eyes to find herself lying in a snow-drift. Her arm ached ferociously, though otherwise she seemed to be unharmed. But her horse had bolted into the night, following Gilmer's fleeing mount. She was alone.

Or was she? For a short way ahead of her, in a clearing, something moved.

Jansie's teeth began to chatter and she couldn't make them stop. The snow was like an icy shroud round her, and only with a huge effort was she able to flounder upright. The bronze sword lay beside her, almost buried in the snow. Dragging it free and taking a grip on it, Jansie stumbled out of the drift and staggered towards the clearing.

She reached the edge – and stopped, transfixed by the sight that confronted her.

Gilmer was in the clearing. He was unarmed and helpless, and his back was pressed against a tree. And, crouched low to the ground with its hackles raised and ears flattened, a huge, black hound – Silvan, the Hound of Winter – was advancing slowly towards him, slavering and drooling.

In a single, petrifying moment, realization of the truth slammed into Jansie's mind. This creature was not the man she loved! It was something else – something unhuman, monstrous; as cruel and merciless as the season after which it was named. And in that same moment she understood Silvan's – the *real* Silvan's – desperation. Though he was transformed from man into beast, a part of his mind still clung to sanity. And he loathed himself. He couldn't be saved. He wanted only to die. And Jansie knew, at long last, the nature of the sacrifice that true love demanded.

She cried his name, her voice breaking in grief. With a snarl the black hound spun to face her, and Gilmer's head turned.

'Jansie!' There was horror in his tone. 'Jansie, what do you think you're doing? Get back – run, Jansie, *run*!'

But Jansie didn't run. In the eldritch snowlight that reflected from the sky and filtered through the pines, she could see the dark shape of the hound with awful clarity. And in the terrible mask of its face, above the dagger-like fangs, Silvan's eyes stared out at her with a tormented, burning plea. He no longer had the power of speech. But the message in his tortured gaze was clear.

Very slowly, Jansie raised the heavy bronze sword and held it above her head. The Hound gazed at the blade, and a strange longing glittered in its eyes. Then it began to pace towards her.

'*JANSIE!*' Gilmer cried. She ignored him. Fearless now, she felt only an ache of sorrow that would burst her heart into pieces. The Hound drew nearer. It no longer snarled, though she could hear it breathing harshly, and its sides heaved as though with some great emotion. Closer. Closer. Jansie began to lower the sword, until it was pointing at the creature's chest . . .

Then she shut her eyes, and with a moan of grief drove the bronze blade into the Hound of Winter's heart.

The Hound made no sound; neither an animal howl nor a human cry. Its slender legs crumpled, and it collapsed panting at Jansie's feet. Blood spilled from the wound the sword had made, staining the snow where it lay a brilliant jewel-red. Jansie dropped the sword, covered her face with her hands and began to sob, 'Oh, Silvan . . . Silvan,

Silvan . . .'

'*Jansie . . .*' The voice was feeble, trembling, but clear. With a gasp Jansie dropped her hands, opened her eyes and forced herself to look down.

The Hound's form was changing. As life ebbed from Silvan's soul the animal shape was slipping away from him, freeing him. He was a man again – but his white, pain-racked face and blood-stained clothes told Jansie that it was too late, far too late, to save him.

'*Oh, my dearest Silvan . . .*' She fell to her knees beside him, tears pouring down her cheeks and mingling with the stained snow. With the last little strength that remained to him, Silvan reached out, and his fingers locked with hers.

'Please, Jansie . . . my sweet Jansie . . .' His voice was weak now; so weak that she could barely hear him. 'Kiss me . . .'

She did. His lips were like frost against hers, and a strange, chill scent hung about him. The scent of death.

'I love you, Silvan . . .' She could hardly choke the words out. But she had to say them. Just once. Just this once.

She saw life flee from him, saw his eyes glaze as his consciousness slipped away for the last time. Jansie cried then, softly, sadly, covering her face and sobbing out her grief with a quiet helplessness. When she could bear to look at Silvan again, his face was calm, the pain smoothed away. He was at peace.

Jansie touched his cheek, very gently, then raised her head. Gilmer stood a few paces away. His body was immobile and his expression filled with sorrowing wonder as he gazed back at her. Very quietly, he said, 'You've released him, Jansie . . .'

Behind him, Jansie saw a pale blur among the trees. Silently the pack of white hounds was materializing, and though in the past Jansie would have been frightened, she felt no fear of them now. They approached slowly, almost

reverently, gathering in a circle around
Silvan and gazing down at him. As one,
they bowed their heads in a last, fond
farewell. They had all loved him, Jansie
thought. Just as she had done.

Soon, like smoke drifting away on a
gentle breeze, the white hounds began to
fade. One by one they became ghosts,
then they became nothing, until only
one was left . . . a creature with blue
eyes. The hound looked at Jansie, and
Jansie felt pain stab her heart afresh as
she whispered, 'Tavia . . .?'

The hound could not speak to her.
But as it vanished Jansie seemed to feel,
just for a moment, her sister's presence,
and across the gulf of death that divided
them she heard Tavia's voice.

'Thank you for freeing us . . .'

Now only Gilmer remained. He held
out his arms to Jansie and she went to
him and wept against the comforting
warmth of his shoulder. With a gentle
hand Gilmer stroked her hair, and said,
'I'll see that he's taken home, Jansie. I'll

see that everything is as it should be for him – and for you.'

Jansie nodded, unable to reply. In a strange, sad way everything *was* as it should be. For Silvan had wanted only release. He hadn't wanted to live on as he was. And however much she loved him, however greatly she yearned for him to live, this had been the only way to bring him peace.

As for Gilmer . . . Jansie knew that he loved her dearly. And although she didn't mirror his feelings, there was a tiny glimmer of hope within her that one day, perhaps, that might change. For a while yet she would grieve for Silvan; but time – as she had thought before – was a great healer. Who could say what the future would bring? There might be happiness. It was what Tavia would have wanted for her, Jansie thought. It was what Silvan would have wanted.

She looked down at Silvan again. When they returned to the house Gilmer would rouse the servants and tell them to bring their master's body home. He would tell them that the Hound of Winter had killed Silvan – and that, after all, was nothing less than the truth. But the real story, the whole story, would be a secret that neither he nor Jansie would ever tell to another living soul.

The snow was falling gently now, glittering in Jansie's hair and rivalling the tears that were drying on her cheeks. Gilmer pulled off his cloak and slipped it around her shoulders, wrapping her warmly. Then he took her arm, and together they turned out of the clearing and on to the forest path.

They did not look back.

Louise Cooper

Heart of Stone

Garland and Coryn have promised to love each other for the rest of their lives. So why is he suddenly so cold towards her? Garland must find the answer to a long-lost secret, or give up the boy she loves for ever.

Heart of Glass

Very gently, he leaned towards her and kissed her.

Aline's dream comes true when Orlando tells her he loves her. But the dream turns into a nightmare when a bitter rival reaches from darknessanother world to snatch her happiness away.

Heart of Fire

Lianne looks into the heart of the topaz and sees the boy she will fall in love with. She also triggers an old family curse. But, good or evil, once she's begun this story, she must see it through to the end.

All available from Puffin now!

READ MORE IN PUFFIN

For children of all ages, Puffin represents quality and variety – the very best in publishing today around the world.

For complete information about books available from Puffin – and Penguin – and how to order them, contact us at the appropriate address below. Please note that for copyright reasons the selection of books varies from country to country.

On the worldwide web: www.penguin.com, for links to Penguin companies worldwide.

In the United Kingdom: Please write to *Dept. EP, Penguin Books Ltd, Bath Road, Harmondsworth, West Drayton, Middlesex UB7 0DA*

In the United States: Please write to *Consumer Sales, Penguin USA, P.O. Box 999, Dept. 17109, Bergenfield, New Jersey 07621-0120.* VISA and MasterCard holders call 1-800-253-6476 to order Penguin titles

In Canada: Please write to *Penguin Books Canada Ltd, 10 Alcorn Avenue, Suite 300, Toronto, Ontario M4V 3B2*

In Australia: Please write to *Penguin Books Australia Ltd, P.O. Box 257, Ringwood, Victoria 3134*

In New Zealand: Please write to *Penguin Books (NZ) Ltd, Private Bag 102902, North Shore Mail Centre, Auckland 10*

In India: Please write to *Penguin Books India Pvt Ltd, 706 Eros Apartments, 56 Nehru Place, New Delhi 110 019*

In the Netherlands: Please write to *Penguin Books Netherlands bv, Postbus 3507, NL-1001 AH Amsterdam*

In Germany: Please write to *Penguin Books Deutschland GmbH, Metzlerstrasse 26, 60594 Frankfurt am Main*

In Spain: Please write to *Penguin Books S. A., Bravo Murillo 19, 1° B, 28015 Madrid*

In Italy: Please write to *Penguin Italia s.r.l., Via Felice Casati 20, I-20124 Milano*

In France: Please write to *Penguin France S. A., 17 rue Lejeune, F-31000 Toulouse*

In Japan: Please write to *Penguin Books Japan, Ishikiribashi Building, 2-5-4, Suido, Bunkyo-ku, Tokyo 112*

In South Africa: Please write to *Longman Penguin Southern Africa (Pty) Ltd, Private Bag X08, Bertsham 2013*